Ghostly Hearts & Body Parts

CADAVER LAB

CAT JOHNSON

Chapter One

THE LARGE BONE, ITS WHITE SURFACE smeared with dirt from what was hopefully many long decades of being buried beneath the ground, didn't seem as out of place as it should resting on the checkout counter at Once Upon a Vine Books & Wine.

That fact served as proof of how much the events of the past months had skewed Natalie Chase's perception of *normal*.

"Liam, are you sure it's..." Natalie swallowed hard as she glanced up at the tall, dark and handsome hunk of man next to her. "...human?"

As she asked the question Mr. Darcy, the shop's resident feline, jumped up to examine the bone more closely. The black cat reached out one paw to poke at the object just as Liam shooed him away.

Once the bone was safe from the cat, Liam's deep green gaze met hers from beneath the dark curl that always rested rakishly low on his brow. "No doubt. It's a femur."

Natalie had to believe him. Not only was he her boyfriend, he was a doctor and the founder of the *Human Institute*—also known as the cadaver lab—located next door.

As much as she wanted him to be mistaken, in spite of the certainty evident in the tone of his answer, chances were slim to none that he was wrong about this.

Surrounding her and Liam and the bone, the usual cast of characters from Natalie's daily life had assembled.

There was Harper, a local author who was Natalie's friend and ad hoc marketing adviser. Jules, the shop's part-time employee. Jules's constant companion Taco the chihuahua, whose bad habit of digging around the old train depot that housed the shop was responsible for the discovery of the femur. And then there was Gabe— the reason Natalie's life had gotten weird enough that she barely blinked over the human remains currently sitting next to the cash register in her shop.

After wrapping up her phone call to the Mudville sheriff's department, Harper lowered her cell and moved closer to the group. "John answered the phone at the department. He said Carson's already in town so he can be here in a couple of minutes."

While they waited, Natalie intended to use the time to question Harper about what she'd said earlier. When Jules had walked in the door, bone in hand and Taco at her feet, Harper had said something to the effect of *oh, no, not again*.

Pinning her with a stare, Natalie asked, "What did you mean when you said, *not again*?"

"Last year some human bones surfaced in the pig pen at Morgan Farm," Harper began.

Ignoring the fact that news had Natalie pressing three fingers against her lips to hold down the nausea that image caused, Harper continued, "Turns out one of the local women tossed her husband in the pig pen rather than pay for a burial."

"No! That's sick," Jules said.

"Well, he had died on top of his mistress so..." Harper bobbed her head to the side with a half shrug.

Liam nodded. "Mmm. Can't really blame her then, can you?"

"Oh, God," Natalie groaned from behind her hand as visions of what pigs could do to a human body filled her mind and turned her stomach.

Liam pulled her closer and rubbed her back. "Just breathe, baby."

"So maybe it's the same kind of situation here," Harper suggested. "Just someone improperly disposing of a body. Illegal, yes, but nothing sinister like *murder*."

"That would be preferable, I guess." Natalie had her fill of murder last year when she and Liam came face-to-face with the man who'd killed Gabe. "But who does this bone belong to?"

Natalie was asking the invisible Gabe specifically while pretending to question those in the room in general.

"Nobody I know of," Gabe answered as the living people, unaware of his ghostly presence, spoke over him.

"Maybe forensics can do DNA testing?" Jules suggested.

"The sheriff's department will look into local missing persons cases, I suppose." Harper shrugged.

Liam, the only other living human who knew about Natalie's recent ability to communicate with ghosts, shot her a questioning glance.

In response she shook her head—the smallest of shakes so no one else would notice—to indicate Gabe didn't know to whom the bone belonged.

There were more resources at her disposal, of course. Those being the other ghosts in town.

One glance out the window told her that word about the bone had already spread to the local spirit community.

The sidewalk in front of the shop was teeming with the curious dead of all vintages. Some more newly deceased like Gabe. Others, judging by the style of their clothing, had been around for centuries.

Thankfully they were all adhering to her rule that no ghosts, save for Gabe, could enter the shop without her invitation.

They remained outside but, like a scene from a horror movie, the hoard of dead peered at her through the front windows. The sight was enough to send a shiver down her spine even after months of her reconciling the fact that this was now her life.

In response to her shudder, Liam held her a bit tighter.

She tore her glance away from the ghostly gathering outside. But the fact remained there were so many, at least *one* of them had to know something about this bone. Or know someone who knew something.

With the deputy sheriff on his way and Harper and Jules by her side, Natalie couldn't make the inquiries personally right now, but Gabe could.

"Maybe we could ask around?" she suggested pointedly with a glance at Gabe that hopefully no one else noticed. "See if anyone knows anything. Remembers anything."

Harper bobbed her head to the side. "I mean I know the old biddies in town are nosy and it seems like they know everything about everyone, but I would think if one of them knew about a body buried behind the train depot they would have said something about it before now. But actually, now that I think about it, it was Alice Mudd who figured out the identity of the bones in the pig pen."

At the second mention of the other bones to turn up just last year, Natalie drew in a breath.

Mudville, at first glance, seemed like a sleepy village. A place where the sheriff's department spent more time enforcing the pooper scooper law than investigating real crime.

Apparently, appearances could be deceiving.

She turned to shoot another glance at Gabe. "So asking around could help."

He sighed as if he had something better to do which, as far as she knew besides eavesdropping on her and her living friends, he didn't.

"Fine. I'll go ask around," he grumbled.

"Thank you—" Immediately realizing her mistake at responding aloud to Gabe, whom only she could hear and see, Natalie stumbled to add, "All of you. Thank you for being here...for me...and the bone."

Liam cocked up a brow and sent her a glance that told her he knew she'd screwed up.

At the same time Gabe shot back, "Nice save, Nat." Then, with a chuckle, he walked right through the door.

As if her day hadn't been complicated enough, she saw past the press of nosy ghosts peering in her window that Deputy Carson Bekker's car had just pulled up in front of the shop.

"Your *friend* is here," Gabe said with a good dose of sarcasm after sticking just his head inside.

"Great." Natalie let out a sigh.

"What?" Harper asked as Jules sent Natalie a questioning glance.

"Um..." She stumbled to explain her outburst. All she could manage was to point at the front of the shop. It had been a long day.

"Ah. It looks like Bekker's here. Natalie and the

deputy have a bit of a *history,*" Liam said, coming to her rescue. With his dark brows raised he shot Natalie a glance, "She did call him to report my being a serial killer right after I got to town."

"In my defense, you had multiple dead bodies stored in your warehouse. I mean who does that?" Natalie asked as she turned to the other females in the room for support.

"How about a *cadaver lab*?" Liam offered.

"Both valid points," Harper said, playing referee.

Liam leaned in and kissed Natalie's cheek. "Just teasing, babe. And don't worry. I'll talk to Bekker. You stay here with the evidence."

"No. Not *evidence*. There could be a perfectly logical and legal explanation—" Natalie called at Liam's back.

They'd already solved Gabe's murder together. She wasn't up for another one so soon.

"Sure. Whatever you say." Liam smiled then turned to open the door.

He headed out as Jules bent to pick up Taco to prevent him from scurrying out the door after Liam, who was one of the dog's favorite humans.

The sea of ghosts, unseen to everyone but Natalie, parted to make room when Liam met the deputy on the sidewalk. The two men had no idea dozens of spirits pressed closely around them.

A shiver ran down Natalie's spine in spite of the heat pumping out of the old train station's big cast iron radiators. She was used to Gabe, but she might never get comfortable with the sheer number of spirits that liked to gather near her at times such as this.

"Don't worry. Carson and the county coroner will get it all sorted out," Harper assured.

Torn, Natalie wasn't certain she wanted it sorted. Nothing good could come of finding bones buried on the property she'd purchased last year.

That thought hit just as Harper's cell vibrated with a text that had her saying, "The LADS are up to take on the case. Agnes offered to host everybody at our place tomorrow night. Six-thirty."

Afraid to ask, Natalie did anyway. "The *lads*?"

"It's short for the Mudville Ladies Amateur Detective Society," Jules answered. "My grandma belongs to it along with her friends."

Natalie felt her brows rise at that information as she pictured the LADS, a bunch of amateur granny sleuths.

Harper must have noticed her reaction and laughed. "Attending their meetings is an experience, I'll admit. You up for it?" she asked Natalie.

"How could I refuse?" Thinking they might need help getting through this meeting, she asked, "Should I bring wine?"

Harper delivered a single enthusiastic nod. "Most definitely."

"Jules, you want to come?" Natalie asked.

A wide-eyed expression of horror crossed Jules's face. "Uh, no. You two have fun though."

Yup. That's about the reaction Natalie expected from her eighteen-year-old employee. She'd probably get the same one from Liam.

She and Harper might be in this thing alone. The sole attendees of this LADS meeting who were under age fifty.

Hell, they'd probably be the only ones below seventy. That might be a good thing for their investigation if the bone were of the same vintage and not more recent. She could only hope the bone was nice and old and no one she knew.

Just when she felt a little better. That they might be able to solve the mystery of the bone in the backyard with the help of the locals quickly so they could all get back to normal—or at least *normal* for them—Liam opened the door.

"Hey, babe. Bekker wants to bring in a crew to dig

and look for more bones on the property. You okay with that?"

She could say no but he'd probably just get a warrant and do it anyway. And then it might look like she was hiding something. She did want to landscape the side yard anyway, eventually. Might as well let them do it.

After drawing in a breath and bracing for the possible discovery of the full skeleton, she forced a tight-lipped smile and said, "Sure."

Chapter Two

Liam stepped up close behind Natalie as she slammed the cash drawer closed after recording the day's credit card receipts and cash sales.

It had been a good day. No more bones had been discovered or brought inside her shop. Considering that alone, today was better than yesterday.

Besides that, she'd made a killing in sales, in both wine and books. Possibly because the local gossip was currently all about the bone found buried behind the shop.

The town gossips and lookie-loos had all stopped by hoping for more information.

While they were there, they couldn't help but pick up a few things, due in no small part to Jules's keen sense for bringing in unique local merchandise on consignment. Not to mention Natalie's obsession with having the shelves fully stocked with the newest and the best books and wine selection at all times.

And now, her hottie boyfriend was here and apparently feeling amorous as he ran his mouth down her throat while his hands pulled her hips back against him.

Luckily she wasn't trying to count the change and small bills left in the cash drawer for the next morning or Liam would have totally thrown her off.

"Mmm. It's six. Can I lock the door?" he growled low and hot against her ear, sending a tremor of need through her.

When had ears gone from being the source of gross wet willies to erogenous zones? Probably about the same time the males in her life changed from annoying boys to hot men.

She was about to tell him she'd already locked the door after he'd come inside so he could lure her into an early bedtime...

A mental record scratch filled her brain and cut her plans short as a memory hit.

"Ah, crud. I promised Harper I'd be at her place right after I closed tonight. She and her aunt are having a group over."

She'd meant to tell him yesterday, but things had

gotten a bit busy between the bone, the deputy and the coroner. Not to mention the locals—both living and dead—who hadn't been able to resist the attraction of two official vehicles parked out front.

Liam groaned again but it was far less sensual this time. In fact, it sounded downright annoyed.

"Blow it off, whatever it is," he suggested, turning her to face him.

"We're meeting to talk about the bone. And since we still have no evidence of whom it belongs to, I can't pass up an opportunity that might provide a lead. You could come with me," she suggested hopefully.

"Uh. Yeah, no, thanks. And just because you can talk to the dead doesn't mean you're responsible for identifying any and all random body parts in the vicinity. Or solving any more murders. There are people whose job it is to do that kind of stuff," he reminded, his mouth pulled to the side unhappily.

"I know, but since I do have a unique... *advantage*, I feel like I should help. You know?" She leaned in to press a kiss to his unyielding mouth before pulling back. "I don't think this meeting will last long. I'll probably be back in an hour. Two max. Wanna wait in the apartment for me?"

Liam sighed. "Fine. I have some articles saved on my phone I can read until you get home. Oh, and there's a new documentary that just loaded I'm interested in."

She'd often wondered if half of the appeal for Liam to hang out with her at her place was the upgraded streaming service offerings she'd indulged in after her unexpected windfall last year. But tonight, if it kept Liam happy until she got home, all the better.

"Thank you for understanding. You're the best boyfriend ever. And the most handsome. And the sexiest." She delivered each compliment with a quick kiss to his face and mouth.

If past experience was any guide, a happy Liam would result in a very happy Natalie later.

Just as her stroking of Liam's ego had earned her a small, crooked smile from her pouty man, Gabe swooped inside through the locked door.

"Ready to go?" Gabe asked as he eyed how closely she and Liam were pressed together behind the cash register. "Or are you and lover boy aiming to get in a quickie before we leave?"

Natalie tried not to read too much into the fact that she *had* remembered to invite Gabe for tonight, something she didn't dare let Liam know.

Gabe would be a useful companion at the LADS meeting. She also wanted to catch up with him on the walk to Harper's place about what his interviews with the local ghosts had yielded.

His help she welcomed. His snarky comments about her and Liam's sex life, not so much.

She turned and shot Gabe a scowl. "Yes, I'm ready to go, smart ass."

Liam pulled back. "I take it we're no longer alone."

"Gabe just came in. He's walking over to Harper's with me."

"Well, isn't that nice." Liam scowled, his comment dripping in sarcasm.

"It's so cute when he's jealous." Gabe smirked.

He moved to pat Liam on the back even though, one, Liam couldn't see or hear him and two, Gabe's hand passed right through.

"Don't worry, big guy. I'll have her home at a decent hour." Gabe's condescending comment went unheard by Liam, who gave an involuntary shudder from the chill of Gabe's ghostly fingers on his shoulder.

Natalie restrained herself from commenting to either one. The sooner she separated the two men—or rather the man and the ghost—the better.

"We'd better get going. Don't wanna be late. See you soon." She kissed Liam's pout then added, "Love you."

"Yeah. Love you too," he mumbled then spun toward the back rooms of the old depot that served as her apartment.

"Aw. He's such a romantic." Gabe clutched his hands to his heart then wiped one eye dramatically. "It brings a tear to my eye."

"Oh, shut up," she mumbled as she slipped the straps of the canvas bag holding two bottles of wine onto her shoulder.

She unlocked the door so she could get out as Gabe slid easily through the window next to her, saying, "Hey, he started it."

"Well, you should be the bigger man and end it," she said as they turned side-by-side toward Main Street.

"I'm happy to be the bigger man." Gabe smirked. "Make sure you tell Liam that. You know, that I'm the bigger man. He should like that."

At that Gabe devolved into a bout of laughter that had him clutching his stomach.

He might not have started the ridiculous rivalry between them, that was all Liam's weird jealousy, but Gabe certainly enjoyed it. A bit too much.

"If you can control yourself from mocking Liam for a few minutes, maybe you can tell me what you found out about the bone."

A woman coming out of the pharmacy turned to

frown at Natalie, who no doubt appeared to be talking to herself.

Tapping her ear, Natalie mouthed, "Bluetooth."

Gabe sent her an indulgent glance at her ruse, and then said, "I haven't found out anything."

Natalie turned her head to glare at him. "Did you at least ask?"

A man across the street frowned at her, probably thinking she was looking at him.

"Of course, I asked." Gabe scowled. "I interviewed every single ghost I could find in town and put out feelers for any outside the village who might know something. So far, nothing. I even tried to ask the guy who got hit by the train. And he has no jaw so that was real fun."

"And? Did he know anything?" she asked hopefully.

Train track guy was perfectly positioned to be a witness. It seemed like he spent most of his time at the probable location of his death, right behind the train depot literally on the tracks. If anyone saw anything, it would be him.

Gabe leveled a less than patient glare on her. "He has no jaw, so he wasn't real talkative."

Natalie scowled, more at Gabe's attitude than the lack of information, although that was annoying too.

"Okay, fine. Thank you for trying." It was time to bring the horrifying jawless ghost portion of the conversation to a close.

This walking and talking plan hadn't been a good one anyway. She was beginning to look unhinged, seemingly talking to herself to anyone who passed her and the invisible Gabe.

Lesson learned. She'd wait to have any future fact gathering conversations with Gabe in private.

Besides their walk had come to an end. The home where Harper lived with her great aunt Agnes came into view.

"That's it up ahead," she said. "Harper and Agnes's house."

"The Queen Anne Victorian?" Gabe asked.

She sent him a brief sideways glance. "Architect nerd?"

"No. Historian, thank you very much," he defended.

"The house is beautiful. Have you ever been inside?" she asked him.

"Hell, no." He shook his head with finality.

"No?" She figured he'd been everywhere.

If she were a ghost, she'd be snooping in all the houses. Especially an architectural gem as beautiful as Harper's.

Gabe shook his head with a seriousness that belied the casual conversation. "Nuh-uh. We ghosts all avoid that one."

She frowned. "Why?"

"It used to be a funeral home."

Natalie discounted that with a flick of her wrist. "Years ago maybe but not now. I've been inside. It's just a house. Nothing to worry about. In fact, it's the one place in town I *didn't* see any ghosts while I was visiting."

"Yup." He nodded. "And that's why. You know any livings who enjoy hanging out in a funeral parlor?"

"Well, no, but—"

"There you go," he said. "Trust me. Funeral homes are no picnic for the dead either."

She rolled her eyes. "So silly. But wait, you are coming inside with me now, right?"

"Yes." Gabe rolled his eyes. "I promised I would and I will."

"Good." She needed back up to listen to all the LADS conversations and see if anyone knew anything.

If there was one thing these women could do, it was talk. Or, more accurately, gossip. But if that gossip led to identifying the bone she'd rest a lot easier tonight.

A bang of the metal knocker on one of the two

giant double glass and wood-paneled front doors had Harper appearing in seconds. "Hello. Come in. Make yourself comfortable. We're just finishing setting up."

"Then you might need these," Natalie said, handing over the bag of wine once they were through the second set of doors that enclosed the front vestibule.

"Perfect. Thank you. I'll put these on the bar."

"Bar? I like this party already." Stepping into the front hall ahead of Natalie, Gabe twisted to take in the twenty-foot ceilings and the grand staircase.

Natalie didn't correct Gabe that this was a meeting, not a party, although sometimes it was hard to tell in Mudville. But she did have to admit that with the big double living room and dining room spaces open to each other, this place probably did make a hell of a funeral home.

Gabe let out a long low whistle. "Okay, I take it back. Maybe I am an architecture nerd. This place is amazing. Look at the woodwork and the craftsmanship on this staircase."

"Beautiful," Natalie agreed softly.

They were both still staring up at the wide staircase that revealed the second floor when a young woman dressed for a fancy party—if that party were a roaring twenties-themed costume party—peeked over the edge and stared back at them.

Natalie's eyes widened along with her mouth on a gasp.

"Uh, Gabe…"

"I see her." Gabe leapt onto the bottom step of the staircase.

That's when the ghost's eyes widened and with a tiny *eep* she turned and ran.

Natalie's gaze followed Gabe as he took the stairs two at a time.

"There goes your rule about funeral parlors and ghosts," she accused softly so Harper wouldn't hear from the kitchen where she'd disappeared with the wine.

"It's more of a theory than a rule," he defended from the turn on the staircase's second landing just as Harper flounced back in.

"Did you say something?" Harper asked.

"Yeah, I was just saying the house is beautiful. One day I'd love a tour."

"We have a few minutes before the LADS arrive. Come on." Grabbing the newel post, Harper started upstairs and Natalie happily followed.

Chapter Three

THE TEXT FROM LIAM ARRIVED ON NATALIE'S cell just as Harper led the way up the grand staircase. The same staircase that Gabe had sprinted up in pursuit of the ghost they'd both seen on the second floor.

HOT DOG

How's it going?

Natalie typed in a quick reply.

Found something!

About the bone?

Not yet. Found a ghost!

An eye roll emoji was all she got back from him.

Admittedly there had been lots of ghosts in her life since that day last year when her heart stopped and Liam had restarted it, somehow linking her with the spirit world.

But after Gabe's lecture about how the local ghost community avoided Harper's house because of its history, the presence of this new ghost seemed significant somehow.

Since Natalie figured she'd better take advantage of Gabe being inside Harper and Agnes's house-slash-former funeral home while she had it, soothing her disgruntled boyfriend was just going to have to wait. If there were more ghosts here Gabe could talk to about the bone, tonight was the night to do it just in case she never convinced him to come back again.

And it would look suspicious if she kept finding excuses to visit the private floors of Harper's aunt's home so she could talk to the ghosts herself.

"The stained-glass windows are all original, but some of the ceiling fixtures are modern replacements," Harper said over her shoulder as she reached the top of the staircase on the second floor.

"Gorgeous." And it was, even if Natalie's mind was not currently on stained glass or light fixtures.

"There are three main bedrooms on this floor, all

three with fireplaces. There's also one smaller bedroom in the back of the house by the servants' stairs that go from the kitchen to the attic. That bedroom I suspect was for staff, if it was a bedroom at all originally. There have definitely been renovations over the years. We can see that. But aside from Alice Mudd's memory, we have to go by the structural clues and some old paperwork the last owners gave Aunt Agnes."

"Mmm. Fascinating." Natalie nodded while keeping her eyes peeled for where Gabe and the female spirit had gotten to.

She followed Harper into the bedroom at the top of the stairs.

"This is my favorite room. Not just because it's connected to the bathroom with the clawfoot tub but because of this." Harper swung a double set of tall wooden shutters wide.

Distracted by the female ghost swooping out of the room with Gabe in close pursuit, Natalie had to force her attention to what Harper had just revealed—a tall glass door that led to a small balcony off the bedroom. Once she did, she drew in a breath.

"This is amazing."

And it truly was. The entrance to the Romeo and Juliet balcony was framed by shutters worthy of

Ebenezer Scrooge's house in *A Christmas Carol*. The door was topped with a stained-glass transom window.

"The bedroom on the opposite side of the house has a similar balcony—" The doorbell sounded below, interrupting Harper. "Oh. Sounds like the LADS are here."

Harper turned toward the doorway through which they'd entered and Natalie knew her tour had come to an end.

Even though the mystery of the elusive ghost was like an itch that needed to be scratched, she followed Harper back downstairs.

Once they'd all gotten refreshments and had been seated, the Ladies Amateur Detective Society meeting went about as Natalie expected it would.

The conversation consisted of lots of women talking over each other, which only got louder as their glasses were refilled.

Finally, there was a lull in the din and Natalie was able to voice her question. "Alice, can you think of anyone who might have buried that bone in the yard of the train station?"

"Well, I can tell you that a year ago I would have guessed it was Ted Simpson buried there by his widow, but of course we found him in the pig pen on the farm. Intact as far as I can remember. The sheriff and the coroner can confirm for you if Ted was missing a bone, I suppose. Besides that, I can't think of another soul who would have the misfortune of being dumped by the train tracks."

"Maybe it's a hobo. He could have died riding the rails and his fellow hobos gave him a decent burial when the train stopped," Mary Brimley suggested.

As Natalie wondered how many hobos had actually *ridden the rails* through Mudville and if train track ghost was one of them, some of the others in the room threw out more theories.

"What about war? Perhaps it's a soldier who died in battle," Dee Flanders, the local attorney who'd handled Natalie's real estate closing, suggested.

"Or who had a leg amputated by a war surgeon," Margaret Trout added.

"As far as local battles, the settlements at Sidney and Mudville were both completely destroyed during the American Revolution." Alice informed them with such an authoritative tone Natalie had to wonder if she'd taught school in her younger years.

"Could it be Native American?" Agnes asked.

"Or one of the workers who helped lay the original tracks," Mary suggested.

The group continued and Harper recorded it all in her notebook, scribbling fast to keep up.

The LADS theories were all over the place and Natalie began to realize her best hope—possibly her only hope—was Gabe and the ghost community.

That was still her opinion later as she and Gabe walked down Main Street toward the train station.

"So?" he asked. "What did you learn?"

"That you should never gather a bunch of women with free-flowing alcohol and no organization and expect to get any definitive answers. You?" Natalie asked.

"I learned that Harper's basement is spooky and I'm never going back down there again, the attic is amazing, there are way too many rooms to search in that house and that woman we spotted, besides being fast on her feet, does not want to talk. Not to me and I'm sure definitely not to you."

Pushing aside the horrifying fact that the basement was too scary even for a ghost, she focused on the girl. "Why do you think she's so spooked? No pun intended."

Gabe shrugged. "No idea. I'm going to ask around the boneyard and see if anyone knows anything about her."

"Ooo, good idea."

He cocked up a brow and shot her a sideways glance from beneath the brim of his ever-present hat.

"Don't get too excited. If she's spent the last hundred years in that house there might be nothing to dig up on her—also no pun intended."

Her lips twitched at their witty repartee. "Touché."

They'd reached the train station and she turned to face Gabe, her keys in her hand. "Thank you for your help and for going with me tonight, in spite of your funeral home aversion."

"You're welcome. I'll keep asking around. And, uh, maybe I'll swing by Harper's house again sometime soon. See if our old girl is in more of a mood to talk when there's not a bunch of people around."

Natalie drew back. "You'd be willing to do that?"

Gabe shrugged. "Sure. You know, in the interest of research."

Suspicious over his sudden change of heart about avoiding the former funeral home, Natalie studied Gabe through narrowed eyes.

"In the interest of research," she repeated.

"Yup." He nodded. "You want answers about the bone, or not?"

Who was she to say no to help when she needed it? Especially from her ghost bestie.

"All right," she agreed. "And now, I need to go. Liam is waiting."

Gabe's eyes lit with mischief. "Say hello for me."

She'd do nothing of the sort. "Good night, Gabe."

"G'night, Nat." With a smirk Gabe sauntered away in the direction of the cemetery.

Natalie turned to unlock the back door of the train station that served as both her work and her home—and apparently also the burial ground for at least one bone.

The county was probably going to start digging up the yard any day now to see if there were more bones. Even with how pitifully unkept it was, having what little grass she had dug up in search of more body parts would suck.

That concern fled when two hands gripped her arms from behind. Then all she could do was scream.

Chapter Four

Her scream bounced off the door she faced until her assailant spun her toward him, cussing as he did.

"Jeezus, Natalie. It's me. Why are you screaming?" Liam asked.

"Why are you grabbing me?" she shot back slapping at his chest.

"I was being romantic." He scowled.

"Romantic! How is scaring the bejesus out of me in the dark romantic?"

"The guys in those romance books you love are always grabbing the heroine."

And he knew that how? She narrowed her eyes. "Have you been reading the books on my nightstand?"

"No. Of course not."

As he avoided eye contact, she didn't believe him but moved on to her next question. "What are you doing outside anyway?"

"The burglar alarm went off in the lab. I had to go check on it."

Her eyes widened. First bones in the backyard and now intruders in the cadaver lab?

"Was there anything wrong?" She sucked in a breath. "Oh my God. No one stole the bodies, did they?"

"I couldn't find anything wrong. And why would anyone steal the cadavers?"

She shrugged, trying to look casual and not panicked at the thought that if someone stole Gabe's body and left town, his spirit would most likely follow.

"Stranger things have happened. You shouldn't have gone inside alone. There could have been someone in there. They could have attacked you."

Liam rolled his eyes. "I was in the Army. I'm pretty good at taking care of myself."

She remembered that trained warrior side of Liam coming out last year against Gabe's murderer. He'd likely saved both of their lives that day. That didn't mean someone couldn't get the jump on him when he wasn't expecting it. That had happened last year too.

"Still, you could have gotten hurt," she said.

There were too many things for her to worry about lately. It was exhausting. When would everything be calm? Normal.

"Thank you for your concern, but it was probably a mouse or something that set off the motion detector."

"Do you have mice in the lab?" she asked, cringing as she wondered if they'd nibble on the bodies. Eww.

Thank goodness there were none in her shop. Probably thanks to her squatter of a cat, Mr. Darcy. At least he was doing something for his room and board.

But apparently, Liam's lab wasn't so lucky.

A lab, by the very nature of its purpose, seemed like it should be kept super clean. At least rodent free. Of course, Liam was working with cadavers, studying the effects life had on the body, so maybe cleanliness was less of a concern.

Liam shrugged at her question. "That building's so old, who knows what's in there. Thanks to you, I do know I have ghosts. Maybe the motion detectors picked up one of them? Although I'm sure Gabe was with you all night..."

She didn't miss the tone of his comment about Gabe, but she couldn't deal with Liam while standing outside the back door. Inside, however, was a different story. There she could use all of her womanly wiles to soothe his ego.

The cold was starting to settle into her bones anyway.

"Can we go in?" she asked.

"Of course." Liam held open the door she unlocked then he followed her in, relocking it once they were both inside.

"We alone?" he asked with a glance around them, not that he would have been able to see what he was obviously looking for. That being ghosts.

She moved and glanced around the shop area to appease Liam. "Mr. Darcy's glaring at us. I'm assuming he's unhappy because we disturbed his sleep. But otherwise, yes, we're alone."

The black cat was stretched out, appropriately, on top of the bookcase which contained the shop's Jane Austin collection.

"Good." Liam took a step closer and pulled her against him. "I missed you tonight."

Wrapping her arms around his waist, she gazed up into the green pools of his eyes.

"I was only gone for like two hours," she teased, even though she absolutely loved that he'd missed her.

"We could have done a lot with those two hours,"

he said, his voice suggestively deep and heavy with innuendo.

She knew that statement to be true and wouldn't mind repeating the experience.

"Then we'd better start making up for lost time." She was just closing in on his mouth when her cell chimed with a text alert.

Liam groaned. "Ignore it."

There are two kinds of people in the world. Those who can ignore a text alert and those who cannot.

"Okay," Natalie agreed even though, while Liam was firmly of the former mindset, she was in the latter camp. No alert should go unchecked.

What if it was important? An emergency. Or not, but if she checked then she'd know that and would be able to continue with Liam with a clear head. With all of her focus on him. He'd want that, right?

As his lips were just about to collide with hers, she pulled back. "Let me just check quick."

He let his head fall back as his hands dropped away from her hips. "Go ahead."

"Thank you. Love you."

"Uh-huh," he grumbled as he turned toward the apartment in the back.

Knowing he'd probably grab a beer from the fridge she kept stocked for him and be fine, Natalie slipped the cell out of her pocket and saw the text from Harper.

HARPER

I found something!

OMG! What?

This!

A picture loaded. A close up shot of dark wood with scratches in it. But when Natalie blew up the image and zoomed in she could see they were numbers. One, nine, two and zero.

What do you think it means?

I don't know. A date maybe?

Rather than a text reply, the cell rang in Natalie's hand and Harper's name appeared.

"Hello," Natalie said as she answered it.

"Oh my God. So if it is a date, the year, that would mean that over a hundred years ago someone stood in this very spot and scratched in the year nineteen-twenty."

"Where did you find it? Where in the house?" Natalie asked.

"The bedroom I showed you. I went back to close

the shutters and because of the way the light was hitting the wood, I spotted the numbers."

That was the same room where the ghost had been hiding. And if it was a year, it was the same era her clothing looked to be from.

"What do you think? Maybe it was one of the kids who lived here back then being bad," Harper said.

"Like roaring twenties graffiti," Natalie suggested.

Wishing Gabe's afterlife came with a cell phone so she could text him with the new revelation, she knew she'd have to wait until whenever he wandered into the shop tomorrow.

Harper sighed. "I would love to know the story behind it. It kills me but I suppose we'll never know for sure."

Or maybe they would...

She remembered Gabe's promise that he would go back to talk to the ghost there.

Maybe with this new discovery he'd be inspired to return sooner rather than later. Or perhaps Natalie could ask Harper to bring her upstairs to see the date in person.

"Anyway, I should let you go," Harper said. "I was just so excited I had to tell you. I know you love this old stuff as much as I do."

"Maybe more." Natalie laughed.

History took on new meaning now she could actually talk to the people who'd lived it. Although Harper had no idea that was why Natalie was so interested and she had no intention of telling her or anyone else.

"And hey, feel free to call or text if you come up with any clues about my bone or the date. Day or night," Natalie added.

Liam wouldn't approve but this was important. They were in the midst of an investigation.

The numbers scratched into Harper's woodwork were intriguing, as was the ghost of the young woman, but the bone in her backyard was the real mystery she needed solved. And something inside Natalie told her it might all be connected.

Chapter Five

Harper's nineteen-twenty woodwork graffiti had been interesting, but Natalie doubted Liam would be all that excited about it. So after disconnecting with Harper, Natalie made her way back to her apartment to find him and get back to business.

The business of *love*.

She smiled at her own cheesy thoughts but allowed herself the leeway to be a little corny when it came to her and Liam's relationship.

Even after these past months and all they'd been through together, this thing between them still felt new.

So new she still expected it to fall apart any day. But also so new she continued to revel in the euphoria of the honeymoon period.

She'd wake next to him amazed it was real and not a dream, and he was in her bed more mornings than not. Not that they were living together. They weren't.

They'd never actually had that conversation. But he'd stopped renting a room at Mudville House months ago. And even though he had a small living area in the warehouse, he spent more nights here than he did there.

She couldn't blame him. They both lived where they worked, but residing in the same building as a wine and book shop was very different than sleeping in the back of his lab knowing the cadavers were just a wall away.

Not to mention the fact Liam's cadavers' ghosts tended to hang around their bodies at the lab.

Not Gabe, of course. His social life was rocking now he was a spirit. But the other two—the older ladies—they were homebodies and barely if ever left the lab as far as she could tell. A fact Liam pretended didn't bother him but she knew it did.

She was fine with Liam being here so much. More than fine. She loved it. And not just because he'd figured out how to bleed the air out of the old radiators so that now they got toasty warm. Or because he was so tall he could reach all the high things she used to have to drag out the ladder for.

It was nice to have him there after a long day of work. To vent to. To snuggle with—Mr. Darcy the cat was *not* a snuggler. To eat with. Watch television with.

Do other things with...

The old train station was plenty large. Enough she'd been able to carve out a decent sized apartment for herself while still having space for the wine and book shop and the room for book club meetings.

Her apartment in back was small by upstate standards, but as large as what she'd rented in the city that had cost her a small fortune each month. The space was more than large enough to accommodate her six-foot plus boyfriend and the big new bed she'd splurged on last year.

When she made her way back to her apartment after the phone call, Liam was sitting on the sofa in front of the television she'd moved from her city apartment.

Captain Kirk and Doctor McCoy were on the screen. Liam had discovered the twenty-four-hour Star Trek channel and though he never forced her to watch it with him when they were together, it was usually what he defaulted to when she wasn't in the room.

She spared barely a glance at the TV before she tossed her cell on the side table and then straddled Liam's lap, facing him.

He dropped the remote on the sofa cushion and planted both hands on her hips.

His dark brow cocked up. "Done with your call?"

"Yes. Done with your *show*?" she asked with as much attitude as he'd used.

"I could be." He smirked. "Why, what did you have in mind?"

"Nothing, if you'd rather watch a fifty-year-old television series," she said while giving just a little wiggle against him.

"Actually, the original series is closer to sixty years old. And don't mock it. A lot of the technology turned out to be insanely on point when considered from a modern perspective."

She sniffed. "Spoken like a true sci fi nerd."

"Spoken like a scientist and researcher," he countered while pressing against her.

After running his lips down her throat, he said, "I would think a romance lover like you should appreciate this show. It can get pretty hot. Kirk was quite the space slut. And then there's that deal with Spock's *pon farr.*"

"If this discussion is foreplay, I have to tell you that your dirty talk needs work." But it didn't make her pull away from him. Not a chance.

He nipped playfully on her earlobe with his teeth,

an enjoyable little habit he did often enough she'd stopped wearing earrings.

The low groan from Liam, combined with the hard length she felt between them, said he'd forgiven her for checking that text and taking the phone call from Harper.

As he moved his hands over her, she didn't even care she could still hear the sounds of the Enterprise's transporter coming from the television.

Her eyes drifted closed at the feel of the heat of his palms as he slid them up her sides beneath her shirt.

It looked like they might not be relocating from the sofa to the bed. That was fine. She'd splurged on new curtains for every window in her apartment when she'd moved in last year so they had privacy.

"Natalie! I have news—"

She screeched at the sound and gave Liam a shove. Leaning away from him she fell off his lap, landing on her butt with an *oomph* in the narrow space between the sofa and the coffee table.

Gabe covered his eyes. "Oh, shit. Sorry. Sorry."

She scowled at him. "What the hell are you doing here? You know the rules."

"Excuse me, but I thought it was safe when I saw the living room light on. Why aren't you in the bedroom if you're going to be doing...*this*?" Gabe indicated the *this* with a wobble of his hands between them.

"I can do whatever I want, wherever I want. It's my apartment. Hence the no ghosts allowed rule."

"I know the rule and I'm sorry. But I knew you'd want to hear this."

Natalie contorted and condensed herself enough to flip over onto her knees and use the coffee table to help her stand. When she was upright and facing back the other direction she saw Liam too was on his feet.

"Hey. Sorry about this. Gabe—"

"No. Say no more." Liam's hand up, palm toward her, in combination with the hard set of his jaw had her abandoning her explanation.

He moved past her.

"I'm gonna sleep in the lab."

Her mouth dropped open. What exactly did that mean? Was this for just tonight? Forever? Was he angry now but he'd get over it? Or were they done for good?

She was still speechless as he mumbled, "Talk to you tomorrow."

Then he slammed the back door closed.

Spinning, she glared at Gabe.

He threw up both hands in front of him protectively, as if she'd actually be able to harm him. She couldn't, even if right now she really wanted to.

"Natalie. Calm down."

"I will not calm down. What if he just broke up with me because of you?"

Gabe cocked up a brow. "If he did then he's not worth your time. Seriously, Nat. If he can't handle the little things, what's going to happen when the big things come around?"

"And this sage advice is coming from a man who died single," she pointed out.

"I'd remind you that he's not far behind me in age and he too is *single. And* he's a man, so maybe I might have some insight you as a woman don't. Hmm?"

She refused to admit he might be right. But between her pulse pounding with fear over where her relationship stood making her lightheaded and the nausea twisting her stomach from the thought that she might no longer have a relationship, she collapsed back against the sofa.

Sleep wasn't going to come tonight. Not with this worry hanging over her head and the growing ache in her heart.

Maybe she could let Liam cool off for a few minutes then go over and apologize.

They'd have an audience in his lab, not to mention she'd have to walk past the body parts that were always laid out on the examining tables, but to not have to endure this sick feeling of uncertainty all night would be worth it.

Until then, she might as well find out why Gabe had felt the need to swoop in here and ruin her life.

With a sigh she said, "Go ahead. You might as well tell me about your news since you're here."

He folded his arms over his chest. "Maybe I don't want to anymore."

She had no more patience for petulant men.

Low and slow in a tone that left no doubt she was at the end of her rope, Natalie said, "Gabe..."

"Fine." As excitement took over he dropped his arms and his expression lit. "The ghost we saw at Harper's. Word around the boneyard is that she was murdered *and* they never found the body."

Well, *that* sure got her attention.

Chapter Six

DURING THE COURSE OF THE PAST YEAR Natalie had uprooted her entire life to move upstate and open a shop, been electrocuted and technically dead for three and a half minutes, started seeing dead people, and been taken captive by a murderer.

None of that seemed as frightening as knocking on Liam's door tonight.

She raised her fist and hesitated. A montage of possible scenarios ran through her head. Most of them weren't good.

Finally, with a "Screw it," spoken out loud to no one she forced herself into action.

Pounding her fist against the metal door, she knocked long and hard.

She wanted no doubt about where she stood with him.

If Liam didn't answer, she wanted to be certain it was because he didn't want to ever see her again and *not* because he simply hadn't heard her knock.

Hearing the deadbolt sliding open had her heart pounding, but she wasn't in the clear yet. He could just as easily tell her to never darken his doorway again rather than invite her inside.

Either way, she'd know soon.

Liam swung the door wide and, looking weary, leaned one forearm heavily on the door frame.

He drew in a breath that expanded his chest beneath the soft white cotton T-shirt he'd changed into along with gray sweats.

Finally he raised his gaze to meet hers.

Breathless, she said, "Hi."

After another inhale, and what felt like an eternally long exhale, he responded. "Hi."

"I'm so sorry," she said in a rush.

His chin dropping, he nodded, before raising his gaze to her again. "I know."

She could make excuses, could try to explain all that was happening, but by now she knew him well enough to believe he wouldn't want to hear any of it.

It wasn't any one thing that had happened tonight

but an accumulation of everything that brought them here. How she consistently prioritized everything besides him—the shop, the mystery of the bone, Gabe—while assuming Liam would just always be there for her. No matter what.

She'd needed to tell him she was sorry, but doing so wasn't enough. She could promise she'd work on balancing everything from now on, but words were meaningless.

Actions spoke louder. She would have to show him she was going to do better. Be better.

But for now...

Natalie flung herself forward, crashing against his hard wall of a chest as she wrapped her arms around his back.

An overwhelming sense of relief filled her when he wrapped his arms around her back and dropped his chin to rest on the top of her head.

He drew in a deep breath and let it out against her hair.

They stayed like that in silence, standing in the open doorway, holding each other tight until Liam said, "Come inside. It's cold."

Regretting the imminent loss of his arms around her she had to admit he was right.

The heat of his body against hers had warmed her but the brisk night air surrounding them was cold.

She nodded and finally, reluctantly, let her arms drop.

Inside, Liam closed and locked the door, then reached for her hand.

Her small, hope-filled smile was accompanied with tears of relief as he laced his fingers through hers.

He led her back past the three steel tables holding various bodies and body parts, covered in sheets of plastic but still creepy, and to a door.

Inside the modest room that he used as his bedroom and living area, Liam turned to face her.

His hands on her hips holding her close as he gazed down at her were a good sign. His silence as he just watched and waited not so much.

"Are we okay?" she asked, half afraid of his answer.

Maybe inviting her in, holding her close, were just his way of letting her down gently while he ended things between them.

They'd been dating for over six months. They were in love. One little fight, not even a fight really, wouldn't be enough for him to give up on them.

Would it?

She hated she wasn't sure.

Finally, Liam said, "We will be."

What the hell did that mean? They weren't okay now?

She'd said she was sorry. She was going to try harder. What more did he want?

The confusion and fear, and admittedly a good bit of annoyance, that she felt to her core must have shown on her face.

Liam drew in another breath.

Letting it out in a huff, he said, "I just had a bad couple of days. We're fine."

"Wait. What happened?" she asked.

How could he have a bad day at the lab? It's not like he could lose a patient. They were all already dead.

"It's just my research." He pulled her closer. "It's fine."

Things were making more sense now. He wasn't one to vent, the way she so often did to him.

Liam was more the kind to come over and try to cheer himself up in other ways after a hard day. Like in bed...

He was getting amorous and she'd left him to go to the LADS meeting with Gabe. And then again when she'd taken the text from Harper. And yet again when Gabe had walked in on them.

"It's not fine," she said. "You had a bad day and I wasn't there for you. And I'm sorry. I'm here now. Tell me what's going on."

"You don't want to know."

"I do. Tell me. What are you working on?"

She tried not to feel bad that she didn't already know the answer. Short of his sawing into Gabe's brain looking for brain damage from his high school and college football days, she didn't know what Liam did.

He sighed. "All right. There's been some exciting documentation coming out of the Veterans Affairs laboratory in Boston from their study of white matter and the effects of trauma from exposure to repeated weapons blasts."

She frowned. "White matter?"

"It's like the wiring in your brain. That doesn't matter. What does matter is that I'm applying for a grant to study CTE in veterans." He took one look at her face and answered her unspoken question with, "Chronic traumatic encephalopathy."

"Mm, hm." She nodded, like that cleared her confusion right up so he'd continue.

"My study *wouldn't* focus on veterans who've sustained a major traumatic brain injury from a single blast, but instead on those who sustained repeated low-level damage over a long period of time. We know repeated blows to the head in athletes can cause CTE, but the Boston findings are the first proof that just being *in the vicinity* of repeated concussive explosions over a long period of time can too."

"That sounds great, Liam." It did, even if she didn't understand it all completely.

"Mmm. It would be if I didn't just hear through the grapevine that another researcher is submitting a similar proposal for the same grant." He scowled.

"Oh. I'm sorry."

"Not your fault," he said, his lips pressed tight into a thin unhappy line. His dimple as elusive as his smile tonight.

"I know it's not, but I'm sorry, nonetheless. I can't pretend I can fix your problem, but I could try to distract you from thinking about it." She pressed closer and rose on tiptoe, putting her mouth closer to his. "If you want."

His eyes narrowed, giving him that dreamy, sexy look that always got to her. Like a shot right to her gut.

"Yeah. I want," he said, his voice low, almost a growl as he began to lower his lips to hers.

"Oh, my. I think they're going to...you know. Do it. Right here."

"Humph. Floozy! She'll regret it. In our day,

women knew you didn't give the milk away for free if you wanted the man to ever buy the cow."

Natalie jumped, startled by the voices of the two old ladies standing inside the room with them.

"True. But I did know of more than one young woman who got pregnant on purpose, just to get that wedding ring."

"Shameful. That girl was lucky. He could have just as easily walked away. Then where would she be?"

"Sent away to the nunnery while supposedly visiting a mysterious aunt's house, only to return months later. I knew one of those too."

The conversation between Ethel and Myra, the ghosts attached to Liam's two elderly female cadavers, might have been amusing had Natalie been observing it at any other time and if the topic of their discussion hadn't been about her and Liam's impending sex.

She tried desperately not to react but she must have stiffened or neglected to respond to his kiss with enough enthusiasm, because Liam pulled back. Then back farther.

He shook his head. "You're not into this tonight."

"No. I am. I really am. It's just..." She paused.

"What?" he asked, his jaw as stony as his gaze.

At the hardness in the tone of that single word

spoken by the man she loved, tears prickled behind her eyes, threatening as she fought to hold them back.

"I don't know what to do. I didn't want to break the mood by telling you that we're not alone. But if I don't tell you, you'll be mad at me again."

"Gabe's here," Liam growled out low.

"No. He's not," she jumped to answer. "It's your two old ladies."

She shot the two pinch-faced women, one in a pastel blue floral housecoat with snap enclosures and the other in a hot pink bedazzled sweatsuit, a quick sideways glance.

"Who is she calling old?"

"She won't be so young and perky herself in a few years."

Enough was enough! Natalie spun on the two ghosts.

"I'm sorry, but you *are* old. One of you literally died of old age. And God willing, yes, I will be as old as you one day. But where are your manners? Why are you standing there invading our privacy and calling me a floozy? You can't tell me your mothers didn't raise you better than this *back in your day*. Shame on you both. Shame!"

She went so far as to waggle her finger at them to emphasize the point.

"Jeezus, Natalie."

Ignoring the insulted *humph* from one of the ladies, and the grumbled, "Well, I never!" from the other, she turned back to Liam in time to see him running one hand over his face.

"Liam. I'm so sorry—"

"No. Don't apologize. And as for those two..." Liam hooked his thumb in the direction in which she'd hurled her rant. "I'm done with them. The truck is coming to pick up their cadavers this week."

"What? He's *returning* us?"

"In a truck! Like we're garbage."

"They will follow their bodies, right? They won't hang around here?" he asked, looking concerned.

With a cringe, Natalie lifted one shoulder. "I'm still learning the rules, but I think so?"

As the ladies continued to complain about Liam's disrespect toward them, a thought hit Natalie. One that had her gut twisting.

"Um, so are you done with just those two or..."

"Don't worry. I'm keeping Gabe," he answered flatly.

Was he keeping Gabe for her because he knew they were friends? Or for his research because Gabe had an interesting brain?

She didn't dare ask why, but relief flooded her.

Meanwhile, the mood had been good and broken now, but she wasn't willing to give up on this night completely yet.

"They're still in here complaining about you 'returning' them. Do you want to come back to my place?" she asked hopefully.

"Yeah. And in the morning, I'm going to call and see if I can move up that pick-up," he grumbled as he grabbed a jacket from a hook on the wall.

"I've never seen such an overt lack of gratitude in my life!"

"I seriously hope one day he donates *his* body to science and gets treated with just as much disrespect as he's showing us."

"Yeah, I think that's a good idea." Natalie nodded in complete agreement with Liam's idea to return the ladies sooner rather than later.

Hand-in-hand, she and Liam headed for the door while she avoided eye contact with the two unhappy specters.

Things were good again with Liam, or at least on the path to getting there. They'd go back to her place and get naked in her ghost-free apartment and all would be well.

Outside as they walked in the brisk night air, with Liam's arm now around her shoulders so the heat of his body warmed hers, her spirits soared—until she spotted the spirit of the train track ghost.

And they were walking straight at him.

Taking into consideration their current speed and trajectory and the ghost's, she estimated they'd intersect in seconds.

Given his messy demise—being hit by a train if she had to guess—and the state it had left him in for eternity—jawless, mangled and bloody—the last thing she wanted to do was walk into him even though she knew they'd pass right through.

Moving Liam was like trying to redirect a barge. She leaned into him hoping to alter their path enough to avoid a collision with the horror headed straight for them.

When Liam proved immoveable she leaned harder, using her body weight and all her might.

That finally worked just in time and she was able to sway Liam two feet to the left. He stumbled in the process, but at least they crossed the track inches behind the ghost, who ignored them as he took his nightly stroll.

After he regained his balance, Liam came to a dead standstill.

Dropping his arm from around her, he turned to face her and frowned. "What the hell was that for?"

It seemed all of her recent problems with Liam stemmed from her ghost ability and her own inability to just ignore it and them. She hesitated and considered her answer.

She could lie and say she'd lost her footing. She was a klutz. He knew that by now. But she was trying to be more honest with him, to have a relationship built on truth and trust. In light of that, there was no avoiding it. She had to tell him.

"We were about to walk through train track guy. I don't even like looking at him. I definitely didn't want us to walk through him. I'm so sorry."

Liam stared at her for what felt like a long time, an odd, hard expression on his face before he let out a breath and shook his head.

"Don't be sorry. *I'm* sorry." He ran a hand over his face—he seemed to be doing that a lot lately around her—then he focused back on her. "Jeezus, Nat. Yeah, the ghosts can be a pain in the ass for me, but I forget how much of a burden this is for you. I'm a selfish bastard."

She took a step closer, resting her hands on his chest. "No. You're just a normal human...who doesn't see the dead. It's okay."

"It's not." He shook his head. "And if I forget again, please remind me."

He covered her hands with his and looked down at her with that panty-dropping gaze that had won her heart even before she knew him. Back when she'd assumed he was a serial killer hiding bodies in the warehouse and even *that* didn't make him seem any less attractive.

"Okay," she agreed. "For now, I can think of a way for you to make it up to me."

A tiny smile quirked up the corner of his mouth. "I can do that."

He glanced up to look toward the back door of the train depot a few yards behind her.

"Is the way clear to the door?"

She looked over her shoulder to check if their path was clear, then turned back to him, happy to report, "Ghost free."

His eyes narrowed with desire. "Good. Let's go."

Before they could reach the back door of the train depot, another man rounded the corner of the building. This one alive.

He lifted one khaki-clad arm to hail them.

"Hello, Carson," Liam said, though his voice lacked the warmth of a usual greeting.

"Liam." Carson nodded. "Natalie, I'm glad I found you. When no one answered the door at the depot I figured I'd check the lab."

"Is there bone news?" Natalie asked, curious in spite of the fact that it was apparent the *mood* was once again broken.

At least this time it wasn't her fault.

Carson nodded. "Can we go inside and talk?"

"Yeah, sure. I'll put on a pot of tea." Natalie sighed and moved to lead the way.

This bone was definitely detrimental to her sex life.

Chapter Seven

"GOOD MORNING," HARPER PRACTICALLY sang when she entered the shop bright and early the next day.

Natalie let her friend's cheerfulness at such an early hour go without comment since Harper came bearing three coffee cups with the Honey Buns bake shop logo on them. She could only handle such peppiness when fully caffeinated.

As Harper put the cardboard cup holder on the counter she said, "You look tired."

Natalie nodded. "Late night. Deputy Bekker stopped by."

Get two former Army men together and it seemed they never ran out of stuff to talk about.

"With news?" Harper asked.

"Yes. Whatever tests the county coroner ran confirmed it's definitely a human bone."

"Which Liam had already told us," Harper chimed in.

"Exactly. But he also wanted me to know that the crew should be here today to start digging to see if they can find more."

"Do you think the rest of the body is here?" Harper asked.

Natalie shook her head. "I have no idea."

"I guess we'll all find out soon," Harper said, looking too excited about the prospect.

"You're going to write this into a book, aren't you?" Natalie asked with resignation.

"Good chance." Harper grinned. "By the way, you have a very vocal raven sitting on your roof right above the front door."

Jules, who was in early to help unpack deliveries, emerged from the back of the store and moved to the counter.

"Hey, Harper. Ooo, for me? Thank you!" Jules plucked out the cup bearing her name in black marker and asked, "What exactly is the difference between a crow and a raven?"

Natalie, finally finished counting the day's starting cash, slammed the vintage register's drawer and turned to gratefully take her own coffee. "Thank you for this, by the way. I need it this morning. And I'm not sure what the difference is, Jules. You'll have to Google it."

"I'm not sure either but raven sounds more literary than crow so..." Harper shrugged, reaching for her own cup.

"Ooo. We should name him if he sticks around. We already have Mr. Darcy the cat in honor of Jane Austin. How about *Poe the crow*?" Jules suggested.

Harper shook her head. "I'm not sure we want this bird to stick around. A very aggressive Blue Jay nested above the back door of Agnes's house last year. He'd dive bomb anyone coming or going. He hit Stone in the head so hard once he bled. I started carrying an open umbrella for protection."

"Besides the threat of potential aerial attack, I'm not sure we have to assign every animal in the vicinity a name. And particularly not a bookish name. Taco the dog doesn't exactly fit into your literary theme," Natalie pointed out.

"Yeah. Sorry about that." Jules cringed. "I didn't realize we'd have a literary theme when I named him."

"I suppose we could go in a different direction for any future animals. This is a book *and* wine shop. Merlot would be a great name," Harper suggested. "Or Chardonnay. Pinot."

"Too bad we don't sell hard liquor. Tequila would be a kick ass name. Right, Taco? Do you want us to get you a friend?" Jules asked the chihuahua at her feet.

"Or Don Julio. Jose Cuervo..." Looking excited, Harper began ticking off possible names.

Natalie held up one hand to put a stop to it. "Nope. We're not getting any more animals around here, nor am I going to start carrying anything more than wine, so no need for more names."

Besides, there was something more important for them to discuss before the day's customers began to arrive.

"Jules, Carson Bekker stopped by last night," she repeated to the girl who hadn't heard because she'd been in the back.

Jules turned to give Natalie a silent wide-eyed stare at the mention of the deputy. Whether that was because he was male stripper hot in his tight khaki uniform or because he might have news about the mysterious bone, Natalie didn't know.

"And?" Jules asked, hesitantly.

"They confirmed the bone is human," Natalie began.

"Which we already knew from Liam, so that's not news," Jules said, repeating Harper's words almost verbatim.

"Yes. Exactly. But what is news is that *today* is the day they're scheduled to start digging up the back yard looking for the rest of her... or him," Natalie rushed to add to cover her error.

She had no proof that the Roaring Twenties girl in Harper's house was the source of the bone. It was just a gut feeling. But one worthy of further investigation.

That was exactly what she intended to do—investigate—but first she had to make sure Carson's excavation project wasn't going to lose her business.

"I think we—meaning you, Jules—need to put something out on social media. Maybe like *please excuse our appearance...*" Natalie suggested.

"*...while we look for the rest of the body parts.*" Jules cocked up on attitude-laden brow. "Something like that?"

"No. You'll figure it out, I'm sure," Natalie said to the cocky teen before turning back to Harper. "We might need another meeting of the LADS. See if anyone found out or remembered anything that could help identify the bone."

"Mmm. I haven't heard anything but the old biddies are never opposed to another meeting so..." Harper wobbled her head. "Sure. We can plan one."

In hopes of getting more time with the ghost, Natalie decided to dangle some incentive. "They might want to take a look at that date scratched in the bedroom at your place, but of course we can meet here if you don't want to put Agnes out."

Jules's eyes popped wide. "What date scratched where?"

"The numbers one, nine, two, zero are carved into the door frame of the guest bedroom at Agnes's house," Harper explained.

"Nineteen-twenty," Jules whispered. "Prohibition went into effect on January first in nineteen-twenty." She glanced up at Harper and Natalie. "We learned about it in school. It led to an explosion of illegal activity. Bootleggers. Gangsters."

That was a subject she was well acquainted with after the events of last year.

Natalie drew in a deep breath and nodded. "Yes. So I've... heard."

She definitely couldn't tell Jules and Harper she'd met a real live—or rather dead—bootlegger last year. Or that the new ghost at Agnes's appeared to also be from that era.

"Interesting that *that's* the date in your woodwork," Jules pointed out.

"But why scratch that or any date into the wood?" Natalie asked, getting the discussion back on track.

"That's the big question, isn't it?" Harper said.

"So let's get the LADS together and discuss it," Natalie prompted again.

Harper nodded. "I'll text Agnes and see where she wants to have the meeting, here or there. Either way, I'll go home and take a picture of the date and tell Agnes to gather all the information she has on the history of the house."

"Perfect." Natalie agreed, while thinking it would be more perfect if she could get into Agnes and Harper's house again to speak to Twenties Girl herself, but she'd take whatever she could get.

"This is exciting. Maybe some gangsters were there at your house!" Jules said.

"Does this mean you'll actually come to the meeting?" Harper asked the teen.

Jules cringed at the suggestion she spend the night with the octogenarians of the town. "I'll think about it."

The tinkling of the bell above the door ended their teasing of the girl and heralded the store's first official customer. Alice Mudd, barely five foot and only if she were to stand up straight, walked in.

"Hey, do you know you have a deranged crow on your roof cawing at everyone who walks by?" she asked.

"That's Poe the crow," Jules announced with a level of excitement that had Natalie groaning.

It seemed they might have already acquired yet another uninvited shop pet. Lovely. Hopefully this one would stay outside.

"Your crow is particularly interested in your landscape crew in the side yard. I'm not sure what they're doing myself. It looks like just a lot of digging. Not that I mind watching them bend over, mind you, but are you putting in a garden, Natalie?" Alice asked.

The bone crew had arrived.

Natalie let out a groan. "No. But actually, maybe." If the holes were already there anyway...

She'd always wanted a formal Victorian garden with stone benches and roses and lavender and a fountain and geometric walking paths between the beds...

One thing at a time.

First, find out if there was a body buried in the backyard, *then* design the garden.

Her To-Do list was certainly getting interesting.

Chapter Eight

THE DISCUSSION REGARDING HARPER'S discovery of those four numbers scratched into the wood of the guest room's door frame, and what they could possibly mean, was the first piece of business of the second meeting of the LADS that Natalie attended.

So far this meeting was proceeding pretty much the same as the first with no apparent organization.

A kind of well-mannered chaos...with refreshments. Except this time, unlike the first, they were in the side room of the book and wine shop since Agnes was having the wood floors downstairs refinished.

That had been a huge disappointment to Natalie.

She'd been hoping to get back there to corner the young female ghost. Especially now, after Gabe had unearthed that rumor about her having been killed and her body never found.

Two things tempered Natalie's unhappiness over the location of tonight's meeting...

One, Gabe had promised to go to Agnes and Harper's house without her—in spite of his funeral home aversion—and try to talk to the girl ghost while the house was empty.

Two, there were homemade cookies from Margaret Trout and a fruit and yogurt dip platter from Mary Brimley. Natalie knew from the book clubs they always offered to leave her any leftovers.

The older generation sure knew how to throw a party—or a meeting. It was becoming apparent that no gathering happened in Mudville without something being served to the attendees.

The treats were accompanied by an urn of very tasty herbal hot tea that was non-caffeinated according to Alice Mudd.

It was perfect for the chilly night and just sipping it had left Natalie feeling completely relaxed. All warm and fuzzy inside.

She was grateful for that. Life had been challenging

lately. She had to treat herself to the small pleasures when she had the chance.

Taking another bite of a lemon-flavored butter cookie shaped like an open book—*adorable*—Natalie leaned back in the second-hand upholstered wing chair donated by Red from her resale shop and listened to the din of voices around her.

"I still say those numbers are a date," Alice said for what had to be the tenth time tonight.

"I'm leaning that way myself, Alice," Harper said from behind the open screen of the laptop resting on her knees.

Agnes, the owner of the turn of the century Victorian for longer than Natalie had been alive, looked down at the contents of a folder. She'd said she'd accumulated the documents over the decades, given to her by various past owners and town locals.

"It looks like in 1919 Evaline Ham sold the house to Fred and Marion Hunt," Agnes read before glancing at the group over the top of the frames of her reading glasses.

"Can you imagine what they paid for that place back then?" Margaret commented.

Glasses back in place, Agnes referred to the paper and answered, "Eight thousand five hundred dollars."

That led to a round of gasps and an in-depth discussion of the value of a dollar and property values before Natalie was finally able to get in her question.

"And when was it a funeral home? What years?" she asked.

If the local dead population was half as gossipy—and inaccurate—as the living, she wanted to gather some facts herself and not just trust the rumor Gabe had heard in the graveyard.

Even though she'd love to simultaneously solve both mysteries—the source of the bone and the death of the twenties ghost—she needed to keep an open mind. Hence, her exploring another theory.

Natalie wasn't sure of all the ghost rules, if there even were rules for the dead, but her thinking was that maybe Twenties Girl might be hanging around the house because that was the place her body had been last—at the funeral home.

If her body had been buried in town but her spirit hadn't moved on to wherever it was those who didn't stick around went, the girl might have chosen to remain in the location of the former funeral home.

"The funeral home would have been about the nineteen-forties, I believe," Alice answered. "The war was on then. Lots of boys leaving for the front. I was very young but I remember Mom complaining that the village variety store ran out of black dye. People in mourning were dying their clothes black."

As Alice spoke, Agnes glanced back down at the papers in her lap. She ran her finger over the page and nodded. "Yes, Alice. Nineteen-forty through forty-four. That would have been the Shermans who owned it then. "

Harper groaned. "Please, can we stop talking about the house's *Funeral Home* era?"

Agnes dismissed her niece's comment with the flick of one hand. "Don't worry, sweetie. You're living on the top floor. The embalming would have been done in the basement and the viewings held on the first floor, I'd imagine."

"Exactly, Agnes." Alice Mudd nodded vigorously. "I remember attending a viewing there when I was little."

Alice Mudd wasn't the town historian but she might as well have been since she'd lived through almost a century of Mudville history. Not to mention Alice's ancestors were Mudville's founding family, hence the name.

Although this town was certainly living up to its name in the amount of actual mud. Natalie's first year here in Mudville had been a messy one. After experiencing heavy rains in the fall, she'd had to invest in big, industrial doormats to contain the mud being tromped into the shop by customers.

After winter's deep freeze had given her hope the mud would remain under control for a few more months, the temperatures had risen enough to melt any snow and ice, leaving the brown mess behind once again.

The spring rains were going to turn her side yard—currently an excavation site—into a hellscape. Taking another sip of minty tea, Natalie decided not to worry about that until later.

"Has anyone found out anything that could relate to the bone?" Harper asked, bringing the LADS back to the real purpose of the meeting, not to mention *away* from the funeral home talk, which really creeped her out given she lived in the house.

The mysterious number slash possible date had taken up the first hour of the meeting and they were still no closer to knowing the reason for it. Although, the discussion had yielded some helpful information. Now Natalie knew Twenties Girl was not connected to the funeral home, but she didn't know much more.

They'd moved back to the topic of the bone and with any luck, some more useful information.

She glanced hopefully around the group, which

had gone silent for possibly the first time tonight except for the occasional clink of a teacup or clearing of a throat.

"Nothing?" Natalie asked, shocked. These people lived to talk. And now they were quiet?

Agnes pressed her lips tight and shook her head. "I'm sorry, Natalie. This bone might have us stumped."

"Maybe those hunks digging outside will find some clues," Alice suggested before glancing around at her fellow LADS. "Did you all see them out there today? Hubba-hubba!"

Drawing in a patient breath Natalie shifted gears.

"What about any killings in town?" she asked, trying to lead them to the graveyard rumor about the murder without actually revealing what she was doing.

"There was the shooting in the parking lot of the Bishop Hotel in the eighties," Mary Brimley supplied.

A bunch of the women in the room, all of a certain age, nodded.

"Any others? Not just recently but over the past hundred years or so," Natalie prompted. "No juicy history of—oh, I don't know—Prohibition era murders, perhaps?"

She glanced around but got only blank stares and a few head shakes.

That was how Natalie's night ended. No answers. No clues.

She should have probably felt more disappointed by that but she couldn't seem to. And on the upside, they'd left her with the leftover tea and cookies.

Chapter Nine

By the time everyone had cleared out and the meeting room was put straight again, it wasn't early but it wasn't late either. Definitely not too late to call Liam and see if he wanted to come over.

Disappointment over the lack of information about the ghost girl aside, Natalie was in a pleasant mood. A mood that would only be improved if she could share it with that handsome hunk of man she was dating.

She picked up her cell and tapped to make the call.

Liam answered on the second ring. "Hey."

"Hey. Whatcha doing?" she cooed.

There was a pause before he answered. "I'm packing away your, uh, two lady friends for pickup. Why?"

Natalie pushed past her macabre curiosity about how exactly one might go about packing up a cadaver for pickup and moved on to the more important reason for her call. "You wanna come over?"

Again there was that pause. Not long, but long enough she noticed before Liam spoke again.

"Any chance you were drinking tonight at your meeting?" he asked.

"No. I mean yes, but not alcohol. We had hot tea. Alice Mudd made it. She said it was herbal and had no caffeine so I had two cups. I'm feeling really relaxed." She felt almost boneless.

Maybe she'd had three cups. She couldn't remember.

"I'll be right over."

There had been no hesitation before Liam spoke this time, or before he disconnected the call.

She smiled at his enthusiasm as she moved to unlock the back door for his arrival. She smiled wider when she peered through the window and saw him striding fast toward her building.

He hadn't even gotten his coat on before he'd left the lab. It remained bunched up, gripped in one hand. The way he was practically sprinting to get to her, he wouldn't be outside long enough to get chilled anyway.

This was how their relationship should be all the time. Liam so filled with want and need he was desperate to get to her. Her single-minded focus being solely on him... Not twenty-four/seven, of course. They needed to have lives of their own and time to work. But dedicating at least a few nights a week to just them would be fine with her.

Liam was nearly to the door when her cell vibrated with a text.

No!

No-no-no-no-no.

She wasn't going to even look. It would only cause a fight if he arrived and she was engrossed in a text. Even if it didn't upset him, whatever it was would definitely break the mood for her.

Nope. She was strong enough to ignore the text and that was exactly what she was going to do.

That decided, she did something she'd never done before. She pressed and held the power button waiting for the cell to power off. Before it did she couldn't help but see Harper's name on the text alert.

She proceeded anyway, holding the button until the screen went dark.

It would be fine. Harper had her aunt and her fiancé to lean on. Not to mention her besties Red and Bethany. And if it was something to be concerned about, Harper would call the sheriff's department or 9-1-1. They'd be better equipped to deal with an emergency than Natalie anyway.

It would be okay that she didn't read the text. It would still be there for her in the morning.

Amazingly, the unchecked text didn't cause any panic. In fact, powering down the cell brought on a sense of relief. Freedom. Anticipation, even. Tonight was for Liam and her alone and that was exactly how she wanted it.

The door she'd left unlocked swung wide and Liam stood in the open doorway. His quick breaths had his chest rising and falling beneath his black shirt. His eyes narrowed when his gaze zeroed in on her.

"Hey," she said, tossing her cell onto the table.

"Hey," he repeated, closing and locking the back door before turning to her. "You have any of Alice's *special* tea left?"

At Liam's pointed question, realization hit Natalie.

It wasn't plain old herbal tea that had her feeling like she was floating on a cloud. Alice Mudd had drugged them all once again!

Alice wanted to share her discovery of the all-natural benefits of ingesting small amounts of magic mushrooms. She thought it would help her friends combat the everyday aches and pains associated with old age and arthritis, as it had helped her.

Micro-dosing the psilocybin was always the octogenarian's—possible nonagenarian since it was hard to judge Alice's age—sincere intent. But *micro-dosing* only worked if the person imbibing stuck to the recommended amount.

One cup. Not many cups.

Natalie had accidentally found that out first-hand last year. Twice.

She should have realized immediately when that first cup had given her the warm and fuzzies. She hadn't.

In her own defense, she had a lot going on right now. And Alice hadn't drugged the meeting beverages since last year. At least not that Natalie knew off.

Be that as it may, it was becoming apparent that once again Natalie had unintentionally over-indulged tonight.

Not that it was a bad thing. She was home, safe, and with Liam.

What a perfect time to take advantage of her altered state.

She and Liam had experienced the effects of Alice's magic mushroom tea together before with some *interesting* results.

Her lips twitched with a smile at Liam's question. She turned and picked up the brimming cup full of tea. She'd transferred the remaining liquid out of the large dispenser so she could wash and return it to Alice tomorrow.

"Want me to heat it up in the microwave—"

"Nope." He strode forward and downed the contents in a few large swallows. Then his hands were on her hips. "We alone?"

"Yes." She wondered if she would have answered differently even if they hadn't been, since the mushrooms were making her not care about much of anything except getting Liam naked.

Luckily she didn't have to test her honesty while she was on shrooms and so happy and horny. Gabe was elsewhere tonight. She didn't know where.

He could still be at Harper's or he could be visiting the cemetery. But right now with Liam's hard body crushing hers she had no inclination to wonder further about her ghost friend's location, as long as it wasn't here.

The corners of Liam's mouth lifted at her answer, then he moved in until his lips pressed to hers as tightly as the rest of him.

The flavor of the honey-sweetened minty tea mingled with the heat of Liam's mouth as he slid his tongue against hers. It had a needy groan rumbling from low in her throat.

"Been a long time," Liam said after he broke the kiss and started backing her up toward the bed.

"Since Alice drugged us or since we—you know?" She tipped her head toward the bed.

"Both," he growled.

She frowned. "It hasn't been *that* long."

"*Any* time is too long." The low timbre of his comment, combined with the look of need in his heavily lidded eyes had her changing her initial opinion and agreeing with him.

"Mmm. You're right. Too long. Let's make up for lost time."

His only answer was to hoist her up against him. She wrapped her legs around him as he carried her to the bed all while kissing her with an eagerness she couldn't help but match.

He tossed her onto the mattress, where she landed with a bounce. His hand was already on the button of his pants, there was determination in the gaze that pinned her where she lay.

His shirt followed his pants and she marveled again at the hard body so beautiful it should be a sin to cover it with clothing.

In nothing but black boxer briefs and looking

worthy of being on a billboard advertising men's underwear, Liam slipped off each of her furry boots, tossing them onto the floor where they landed with a thud.

He reached for the elastic waistband of her leggings. In one brisk move, he tugged them and her underwear down her legs. They landed on the floor as well.

Then he was between her legs, slowly crawling onto the mattress, his eyes on her like he was a predator and she was his very willing prey.

Her stomach twisted with need and her mind spun. Liam was right. It had been too long. They should be doing this all the time. Day and night.

He lowered his head and the heat of his tongue hit her, the sensation immediately shooting straight to her core. She cried out as her hips jerked to meet his mouth and her eyes slammed shut.

When she forced them open she found herself captured by Liam's intense green gaze.

She couldn't keep her eyes open for long. This man knew exactly how to touch her. How to take what was good and make it even better.

He made her wonder who was in control of her body. It didn't seem like she was any longer as it did things she had no control over.

Muscles tightened and then that tension broke free with a frightening intensity.

Breathing seemed harder than it should as he pushed her body to the brink. To the point where pleasure bordered on pain. Until she used the hands that gripped Liam's hair to push him away when she couldn't take any more.

As she lay panting, she managed to pry her eyes open. It was worth the effort when she was treated to that crooked smile she'd been missing.

He rose on his knees and ran one hand across his mouth. Then his eyes narrowed as he moved over her saying, "Catch your breath, baby, because I'm not nearly done yet. We're just getting started."

It was going to be a good night.

She'd have to thank Alice tomorrow.

Chapter Ten

Under the flannel sheets and thick fluffy comforter, Natalie's bed was toasty warm.

The heat of Liam's bare body pressed up against her back penetrated even through the fabric of the bralette, long-sleeved T-shirt and underwear she'd pulled on last night to sleep in.

She and Liam had finally worn each other out sometime close to midnight.

Now, she was in that happy state between sleeping and waking. A place where she'd give anything to remain forever.

She was so comfortable she couldn't imagine moving a muscle. And since the alarm hadn't gone off yet, she didn't have to.

Holding on to the enjoyment, she treasured every moment.

"Um, hello. Natalie. You alive?"

Gabe's voice yanked her out of her bliss and fully into consciousness.

Her eyes flew wide and she glared at him without moving, without speaking, in an effort to not wake Liam. Or worse, alert him to Gabe's presence in her bedroom, while they were still in bed.

Things last night had been too wonderful. Gabe's intrusion and Liam's reaction to it would ruin everything.

Gabe held two hands up, palms out defensively. "I know I'm not supposed to be in here. But I was worried about you. Harper is outside freaking out. She's on the phone calling Jules to bring over the spare key so she can get in to check on you."

Natalie frowned. What was wrong? Why was everyone so worried about her? It was still early.

As if reading her mind—or at least interpreting her expression of confusion since she seriously hoped Gabe couldn't read her mind—he said, "You're thirty minutes late opening the shop."

But her alarm hadn't even gone off yet—

Oh, no. Her cell phone.

She'd powered it completely off last night. Her alarm *couldn't* go off.

Shit! She flung the covers off, ignoring Gabe as she reached for the pair of leggings still on the floor where Liam had tossed them when he'd undressed her last night.

She pulled them on over her underwear then reached for the *Book Nerd* sweatshirt folded on top of the pile of laundry she had yet to put away. She tugged that on over the T-shirt she'd slept in and searched the floor for her boots. All without saying a word to Gabe.

Unlike Liam, Natalie couldn't sleep in the nude. The few times she'd tried, she'd had dreams all night that she was out in public naked in the most inappropriate locations. Like in the shop. Or on Main Street. She usually slept in nearly as many clothes as she wore to work.

Even so, there was no doubt in her mind that Liam would consider Gabe standing there while she got dressed inappropriate, so she had no intention of telling him that's what was happening.

"What's going on?" Liam asked, his voice groggy as he woke.

She spun to locate her useless cell phone. "I overslept. I have to open the shop. It's late."

He groaned and moved to flip back the covers which would have given Gabe an eyeful.

"No! You can stay in bed if you want. No rush. But I gotta go. Love you. See you later. Bye." She shot Gabe a *time to go* glare and rushed toward the door.

Gabe snorted behind her.

"Don't worry. I don't need the blow to my ego I'd get from seeing naked Casanova back there. I mean it's not like I can go pumping iron to get some of those ridiculous muscles like his. I'm destined to remain how I died, and I was a little too busy searching for the treasure of a lifetime to join a gym, so sue me..."

Gabe continued to grumble as Natalie skidded into the shop area.

She could see Harper standing outside the locked glass door, cell pressed to her ear, just as Gabe had said.

"Sorry!" Natalie called through the glass while twisting the key in the lock.

"Never mind, Jules. She's here," Harper said then disconnected the call as Natalie pulled the door open.

She repeated the apology as Harper walked inside. "I'm so sorry. My alarm didn't go off."

"Phew. No, it's fine. I was just worried. When you didn't even read my text from last night and then didn't open the shop today—"

"Yeah, my cell was dead. Sorry," she said, lying as

she reached back and flipped the sign from *Closed* to *Open*.

She moved behind the counter and made a show of plugging in the cell and turning it on. The phone's display showed it wasn't completely a lie. She hadn't charged it last night after turning it off so it was close to dead now.

"What was the text?" she asked as she turned back to Harper, who'd followed her to the counter and stood—unknowing—next to Gabe.

"I think Agnes's house is haunted," Harper announced.

Natalie's eyes flew wide as Gabe drew in a breath.

"Yeah, that's the reason I stopped by this morning. I might be responsible for that." Cringing, he indicated the distraught Harper next to him.

Dragging her attention away from the invisible man and back to her friend, Natalie asked, "Why do you think the house is haunted?"

"Besides the fact it used to be a funeral home?" Harper asked then continued. "Strange things happened last night."

Natalie cut her gaze to Gabe then back to Harper. "What kind of strange things?"

"The sound of footsteps for one. And then there's the stuff in the attic."

"You live in the attic," Natalie reminded.

"Yes, but Stone walled off a storage area up there, separate from my bedroom. It's where Agnes keeps all the Christmas decorations. Last night, one of the small tabletop trees fell over."

"Maybe it was vibrations, like from you walking, that knocked it over? Or even the train."

The freight trains that still ran on the tracks vibrated Natalie's place day and night. The tracks were close enough to Main Street to vibrate Agnes's house too.

"No. It was me," Gabe admitted. "Fun fact, I apparently can knock things over now."

Good thing Harper was completely distracted by her fear that Agnes's house was haunted or she might have noticed Natalie looking shocked as she stared at Gabe.

This was a huge revelation. Was Gabe always able to do that or was this a new skill that grew with time? Did any of the other ghosts have abilities? She had so many questions. None of which she could ask now.

"And then—Stone thinks it was the wind but I'm sure it wasn't—I heard a *voice*," Harper said, looking pale.

"A voice? What kind of voice?"

"A man's voice. I swear he said, 'Please talk to me'."

Gabe ran a hand over his face then leveled his gaze on Natalie. "I was trying to talk to the girl. I managed to grab her arm, but she ran again. I guess Harper can hear me now too."

"This is amazing," Natalie said, before realizing she'd spoken aloud.

"Amazing for you, maybe. You're not living in a haunted house." Harper's tone raised a solid octave on those final words as she leaned heavily on the counter.

Natalie was going to have to discuss this turn of events with Liam. Even though her boyfriend had no love for her ghost bestie, he'd have to be interested in this new development in Gabe's abilities. Just from a scientific standpoint. Liam was first and foremost a researcher, after all.

She'd also have to discuss this further with Gabe later. Right now, it was time to concentrate fully on her living friend, before Harper passed out right there in the store.

"Harper, I'm sure—"

"That I'm imagining it?" Harper finished for Natalie. "That's what Stone and Agnes think."

Natalie shook her head. "No. That wasn't what I was going to say. If it is a ghost, as you suspect, I believe that whatever—whoever—you encountered is harmless. It's scary, yes. I understand that. But it—he

—wasn't there to hurt you, I'm sure. He's probably just a poor soul who hasn't moved on yet."

Harper's eyes widened. "You believe in ghosts? You don't think I'm crazy?"

A year ago her answer would have been different, but given the circumstances… "I believe you."

"So what do you think I should do?" Harper asked.

"Nothing. You've lived there for a few years now, right? And this is the first time something like this has happened?"

"Almost five years, but if it happened once—"

"I think it's probably a one-time thing. I mean, once in five years. It's probably a fluke. I bet it won't happen again." Natalie shot Gabe a glance as she laid a hand on Harper's shoulder.

"We can't know that. What if it keeps happening?" Harper asked, no less flustered in spite of Natalie's attempt at assurance.

"If it does, you call me right away. I'll be there for you. But I do think you have nothing to worry about."

Harper pressed her lips together. "All right. But I'm going to hold you to that. You keep that cell phone charged from now on."

"I will. Promise."

Harper drew in a breath and let it out. "All right. I'm heading home. I have research to do."

"Good. Don't let last night keep you from your normal work schedule."

"Oh, there's no work happening today. I'm going home to grab my laptop and take it to the library. I'll use their WiFi. I need to research hauntings. I'll let you know what I find out."

Oh, boy. When Harper started researching she really went down a rabbit hole. But at least it would keep her busy so Natalie could talk to Gabe alone. "Okay. Text me later."

"I will."

Once the door had closed behind Harper, Gabe chuckled. "Joke's on her. There are at least half a dozen ghosts who like to hang out inside the library."

Natalie spun on Gabe. "What the hell? You have ghost powers now? Did you always have them? Or did you like come into them now you've been dead a while? What's going on?"

He shrugged. "I don't know. You know as much as I do at this point."

"I feel like we need to test this. I'm going to get Liam."

His brows rose beneath his hat. "If you think that's a good idea."

"It's my only idea. Who else can I ask to help us test your new powers? It's got to be Liam."

"Did I hear my name?" Liam asked as he wandered out of the back, two cups of coffee in his hand.

He glanced around the shop.

"And given that you're alone, I'm going to assume I should say good morning to Gabe. Sorry I can't bring you a coffee, bud." Liam didn't look at all sorry as he handed Natalie her cup then took a long and overly loud slurp from his own before letting out a big, satisfied sigh. "Mmm-mmm. So good."

Gabe rolled his eyes. "Tell lover boy I'm a tea drinker, but thanks a lot. Nice way to try to torture the dead."

"Tell him yourself," she said.

"What?" Gabe frowned. "Why are you being mean to me too?"

"I'm not. I meant try to talk to him. Harper heard you. Right? Maybe Liam can."

"Wait, what? Harper can hear him now?" Liam asked looking a little pissed about it.

"She did last night." Natalie turned back to Gabe. "So try."

The ghost drew in a breath and let it out, even though she didn't think ghosts actually breathed.

"Okay, fine. Hey, Liam! Does Natalie know you do

your pushups to a Taylor Swift playlist? He sings along to *Shake it Off*," Gabe added as an aside to her.

Ignoring that information, which was actually news to her, she turned to Liam. "Well? Anything?"

Liam shook his head. "Nothing. What did Harper hear?"

"Gabe was in the house trying to get that new ghost we discovered to talk to him and Harper heard him. She also heard his footsteps. *And* Gabe actually knocked over a Christmas tree stored in the attic." With a new idea, she turned back to Gabe. "Try touching something. Knock it over."

"Nat. I walk through things all the time and I never knocked anything over before."

"Just try. Something easy. Like this card." She grabbed a notecard she'd pinned to the bulletin board and stood it on the counter. "See if you can knock that over."

"All right." Gabe moved closer and swatted at the card. His hand passed right through.

"Try again. But concentrate this time."

"Not sure why concentrating would help. I wasn't concentrating last night. I just bumped into the damn tree when I grabbed the girl."

"Come on. Just do it."

"Fine." With a huff, he leaned low and stared at the object.

Frowning, he reached out and, moving more slowly this time, he touched it with one finger.

Again, nothing happened except for his finger passing right through.

He straightened and said, "Nope. Can't do it."

Natalie let out a sigh.

Liam cocked up a brow. "No good, I'm assuming."

"Correct."

"Well, this was fun. I'm heading to the lab. The body donation program folks are coming to get your two friends, Gabe. So if you want to say goodbye to them, you'd better do it now."

"*Humph*. Chops them up and then sends them back. When's he going to ship me out, I wonder? Or does he have more sawing to do? The latest is he's slicing my brain into the thinnest slivers I've ever seen. Can you imagine what it's like to see your own brain on a slicing machine like it's a roast beef at the deli counter?"

"Gabe says thanks for letting him know," Natalie lied, which had Gabe shooting her a glare before he stalked through the wall and outside.

"My pleasure," Liam said with a smile before he leaned in and gave Natalie a kiss. "Talk to you later."

"Yup." She watched him go and then stared around her wondering what to do as she found herself completely alone for the first time since waking that morning.

Going from too much company to none at all was disorienting...but not as much as the raven that landed on the window box outside the front window to stare at her. Like *really* stare at her as if he had something important to say.

And damned if Mr. Darcy the cat didn't move a muscle as he continued to sleep in the sun shining on the windowsill inside, just a pane of glass away from the bird that nature dictated should be his enemy.

The problem was—aside from her useless cat—what if this creepily intense raven did have something to tell her?

Stranger things had happened.

She turned away to drink her coffee. If the bird did want to tell her something, she was fairly certain she wouldn't want to hear it.

Chapter Eleven

"Hey, Gabe?"

"Yes, Natalie?"

"What do you know about crows?"

He cocked up one sandy brow. "Um, I know a normal amount I guess. Why?"

"That crow on the roof—"

"The annoying noisy one." He nodded.

"Is it possible he's like, I don't know, a messenger?"

There went that brow again, flying up until it was invisible beneath the brim of his hat. "A messenger from..."

"The beyond?" Her answer sounded more like a question.

After the look of surprise left his face, he said, "I don't know. I don't think so."

"Could you ask?"

"Where exactly do you think I'm supposed to get these elusive answers to all of your many and varied paranormal questions?" Gabe asked.

Natalie shrugged. "I figure you crowd source the answers from the spirits in the graveyard. Am I wrong?"

"No. Not really. But there's a limit to what they know. Even the older ones. And it's not like there's a ghost manual. Or a ghost library. Or even a living library with a ghost librarian. You know?"

"Yeah, I get it. Could you just try?"

"Yes, Nat. I'll try. And why do we think this crow is a *messenger from beyond*?"

Ignoring the attitude in his question, she answered, "He seems desperate to get my attention. Staring at me through the window. Screaming from the roof above the door."

"Just be glad he didn't bring a *murder* with him." Gabe grinned, looking pleased with himself. "Get it? A murder of crows. That's what a group of crows is called—"

"I know. Yes, I get it." She rolled her eyes. "Very clever. However, given the bone in the yard, murder is a bit of a touchy subject around here right now. Don't you think?"

Natalie's plate was more than full thanks to that damn bone.

The holes from the crew still digging up the yard were getting bigger and more numerous. In an effort to not panic, she had become obsessed with garden designs on Pinterest. That was when she wasn't searching the internet for the best species of shrubs and ornamental trees for this region.

Not that she had a whole lot of spare time for garden plans. Jules called in sick after the doctor confirmed she'd succumbed to mononucleosis at college. That meant Natalie had lost her only relief at the shop for the next week.

Even though the teenager was only part time, even if she relieved Natalie for just a few hours it was an enormous help. Especially on book club nights. Jules coming in for a couple of hours meant the difference between Natalie getting to pee and eat a meal versus her having to work ten straight hours with no breaks at all.

And Natalie had to make time for Liam. She *wanted* to spend time with him. Of course, she did. Just sometimes it was hard given her schedule.

Then there was dealing with Gabe and the rest of the ghosts, which took up a considerable amount of mental energy.

She'd gotten to the shop early just to grab some time alone with Gabe and catch up before people started arriving. Obviously that had backfired because Harper was now standing outside the locked glass door.

"Looks like our little chat is over," Gabe commented. "Guess I'll go start on my *crow homework*."

"Thank you," she mumbled, trying not to move her mouth as she approached the door and Harper.

"I live to serve... or... you know what I mean," the ghost joked as Harper blew in through the door Natalie pulled open.

"I heard it again. The ghost. Last night," Harper announced, eyes wide with panic.

"Uh, oh." Gabe had begun backing out of the building when Natalie's glare stopped him.

Any doubt that it had been Gabe that Harper heard was dispelled by his guilty expression.

"What did you hear?" Natalie asked Harper while trying to maintain a soothing tone.

"Footsteps again. Voices. Two this time. One sounded female, although I couldn't make out any words—especially after I ran out of there. I spent the night downstairs in the guest bedroom. Not that I could actually sleep. Stone thinks I'm ridiculous. He slept through the whole thing and then stayed upstairs in bed without me. So there goes your theory that the other night was a one-time thing."

"Yeah. I guess I was wrong." She shot one more glare at Gabe for being careless.

Now that it seemed he had the strange ability for at least Harper to hear him, he was supposed to try to get ghost girl to talk while no one was home. Not while Harper was right there.

"But I wasn't wrong that it's harmless, right? Stone was fine upstairs. And it didn't hurt you," Natalie added.

"No, but..." She shook her head. "I'm not sure I can live like this. I'm ready to buy a camper and move to the back yard. A nice new RV so there's no chance of it being haunted."

Natalie kept to herself that she didn't think Harper's idea for ghost-free living would work. She was pretty sure Gabe could just as easily walk into a new camper as an old house.

She was just thinking of what to say to reassure Harper, while trying to figure out how to get alone again so she could interrogate Gabe, when Harper's cell phone rang.

Harper glanced down at the screen. "Ooo. I have to take this."

As she moved toward the meeting room to take the call, Natalie spun to Gabe.

"What the hell?" she mouthed.

He spread his hands wide. "I'm sorry, Nat. When I finally got her to stop running away from me I didn't want to leave. She actually talked to me."

"And you didn't tell me?" Natalie whispered after a quick glance at Harper to make sure she was still distracted by the call.

"I was going to..."

Natalie crossed her arms and narrowed her eyes. "At least tell me what she said."

"I'm trying to gain her trust. She's started to talk to me—a bit—but the moment I bring up her death, she clams up and runs away again. It's been slow going but I haven't given up."

Natalie drew in a breath and nodded. "Okay, b—"

"Oh, sorry. Are you on the phone?" Harper asked, surprising Natalie from behind before she could reiterate to Gabe that he had to *be careful.*

She turned to face her friend as she searched for an excuse as to why she was speaking to seemingly no one. "Uh. Nope. Just talking to myself. Little pep talk before I start the day. *Okay. Be great today.*"

Harper's dark brows rose. "Good plan. I could use a little pep talk today too after getting no sleep last night. Or the night before. But hopefully this will all be over soon."

Interest piqued, Natalie asked, "How? What's your plan?"

Was she serious about that camper she'd mentioned?

"That's what the phone call was about. I've done a lot of research and I know what I need to do. It doesn't matter whether Agnes or Stone believe me or not, because the person on the phone does. And they've agreed to help."

"Help how? By doing what?" Natalie asked.

"An exorcism," Harper announced.

Chapter Twelve

At hearing that one word—exorcism—Gabe's gasp matched Natalie's.

He swayed and reached for the doorframe to steady himself...and fell halfway through the door.

After he righted himself, he locked his gaze on Natalie. "Nat. Do something."

She could see the fear in his eyes. Hear it in his words. She couldn't blame him.

What would an exorcism do? To the ghost girl in the house. To the spirits in the surrounding area. To Gabe...

Or maybe it would do nothing at all.

Latching onto that hope, Natalie asked, "Do you think exorcisms work?"

Unless she could talk Harper out of it, she supposed they were all going to find out.

Harper pursed her lips and bobbed her head to the side. "There are some compelling writings to support that they do. Particularly about the man who was the Chief Exorcist of the Diocese of Rome. All I know is I have to do something if I ever want to step foot in Agnes's house again without shaking with fear."

Loyalties torn, Natalie stood, speechless, her head spinning.

Poor Harper appeared genuinely frightened. But she needn't be. The ghosts—so far, anyway—had proven themselves to be harmless. Annoying, yes, but not violent or malevolent.

Gabe looked as frightened as Harper. Scared to death—so to speak. But he'd brought this situation on himself. He'd returned to the house after it was clear he shouldn't.

Meanwhile Natalie had a slew of questions. Who in the world had Harper gotten to agree to perform an exorcism? How had she found them?

More, how the hell much did a home exorcism cost?

This area seemed ripe for exploitation by scammers who charged a fortune for a job that had no proof of completion. Natalie would be able to tell if the ghosts were gone but who else could? No one as far as she knew.

That brought up another consideration. Was this person also able to see and hear ghosts like her? She wasn't sure how she felt about that. She was torn between wanting to speak to a kindred spirit about the challenges of her new ability versus not trusting another human enough—aside from Liam—to even start that conversation.

There were so many questions but no answers as Harper shoved her cell into her pocket and said, "I have to get home and convince Agnes to let me do this at her house. Otherwise, and I hate to even say this, I might have to do it during the next book club meeting when she's here with you so she doesn't know. I'm sorry to bring you into my possible deception, but I'm desperate."

Natalie didn't know what to say, so she nodded. "It's okay. I understand."

"Thank you. I'll let you know how it goes."

After Harper strode out of the shop, Natalie spun to Gabe. "Now look what you did."

"I know. I know. It was stupid. I just didn't think she'd hear. I was so careful. I literally tiptoed so she wouldn't hear me walking. I didn't bump into anything this time. I didn't talk to her in the bedroom.

We were in the damn closet and I was whispering. I don't know how she heard—" His eyes widened. "Hey, wait a minute. How can she hear me there and not here? I was talking to you with her in the shop."

Natalie frowned. "You're right. You did talk to me and Harper didn't seem to hear you at all, but she obviously hears you there in the house. Why is that?"

"It could be location specific."

Natalie jumped at the sound of Liam's voice behind her. "Jeez. You scared me."

"Sorry. I used my key and came in the back door."

"Why? The front door is open."

"I ran out of coffee at my place. I thought I could sneak in, grab some and leave." He cringed. "Sorry. I'll replace it. I just didn't want to take the time to run to the store this morning."

"Don't worry about it. I get mine auto delivered every month."

"Of course you do." He rolled his eyes over her aversion to grocery shopping. "But back to this Harper thing..."

"Yeah. What he said," Gabe agreed.

"I suppose we need more experimentation," Liam continued.

"Such as?" she prompted.

"Such as can other living people hear Gabe in

Agnes's house or just Harper? Is it the entire house or just Harper's bedroom or the attic or wherever? Location specificity is an extremely interesting concept. That there might be something in that exact location—electromagnetic fields, mineral deposits—that make ghosts able to be heard is a fascinating theory."

Gabe let out a grunt. "He's getting all science-sy again."

"Yeah, I know. It's annoying when he talks science but also kind of sexy, right?" she asked.

At that, Gabe groaned and Liam rolled his eyes.

"So what do we do?" Natalie asked bringing them back to her and Gabe's main concern. She realized Liam wasn't up on all that was happening and added, "Harper is planning an exorcism at Agnes's house."

Liam lifted his brows at that. "What will that do to them?"

"That's what we don't know. Do you?" she asked Liam.

"No. This isn't exactly my field of study."

"Great." Gabe scowled. "Where's all his sexy science now that we need it?"

Natalie didn't pass on the comment as Liam got a familiar look on his face. A slight frown crossed his brow and his eyes seemed to lose focus as he stared past her at nothing while stroking the stubble on his chin.

She knew Liam well enough to know what this posture meant.

"Hang on. He's thinking," she told Gabe.

"You think? I thought maybe he was posing for a portrait." Gabe scoffed.

"There's no need to get snarky. We're trying to help you."

"Oh, you can help me. You just refuse to."

"How can I help you? And when did I ever refuse to do anything you asked? Anything reasonable, that is?"

Gabe leveled a stare on her. "You could tell Harper everything. How you can see us since you got electrocuted. How we're friends. How I was only in that damn house to get information for *you*."

He was right. On all counts. Including the fact this was the one thing she could do for him that she couldn't bring herself to.

"That might not even work. Even if Harper knew everything, it doesn't mean she'd change her plans."

"You don't know that. I think she would. In fact, I think she'd be all over it and probably write a book about it," Gabe said.

"Oh my God, you're right. She totally would write a book about it."

And that right there made Natalie's decision even more firm. She could never tell Harper about her ability or the whole world would know.

Natalie shook her head. "No. I can't do it. I'm sorry, Gabe. We'll come up with another solution. I promise. I won't let Harper banish you or any of the others to... wherever."

Where would they go? Heaven? Hell? Some sort of purgatory on another celestial plane? She swallowed hard at the thought.

"We'll figure it out. You can convince Twenties Girl to leave the house. She can hide out here or somewhere else. Wherever she's comfortable. I really don't think exorcisms have the power to clear a whole town, if they work at all. I'll research that, okay?"

"Okay." Gabe blew out a breath.

As they'd discussed the situation and possible solutions—anything aside from her telling Harper—Liam had taken out his cell phone and was busy tapping and scrolling on the screen.

"It looks like Casanova has an idea. How about you ask him?"

She nodded. It was the least she could do for Gabe.

She cleared her throat. "Um, babe. Do you have an idea?"

He nodded, slowly at first and then more excitedly. "Yeah. I do. Can you get me inside Harper's house?"

"Uh, yeah. I don't see why not."

Harper was so desperate about this haunting situation that she wouldn't say no to a scientist wanting to help.

Liam nodded again. "Good. I'll need Gabe there too."

"Not a problem," she answered with a quick glance at Gabe who agreed with a tip of his head. "What are you going to do?"

"Live out at least one of my childhood fantasies."

Baffled and more than a little curious, Natalie asked, "And, um, what is that?"

"Becoming a ghostbuster." Liam grinned. "I gotta go. I might need to buy some equipment. Ask Harper!" he shouted at her over his shoulder as he disappeared into the back.

Natalie shot Gabe a concerned glance.

Had they just jumped from the frying pan and into the fire?

Chapter Thirteen

Loaded down with numerous unidentifiable devices hanging on him by various straps and bags worn over his normal clothes, Liam looked less like the *Ghostbusters* from the Bill Murray/Dan Ackroyd movie and more like all those supposedly real ghost hunters on television.

"If there are any ghosts with us here today, can you say something?" Liam asked. Then he waited while diligently staring at the device in his hand.

When nothing happened, Liam raised his gaze to shoot Natalie a wide-eyed glance.

She in turn delivered a similar glare at Gabe, who sighed but complied by saying, "Testing, testing, one, two. Houston, we have a problem. Today is a day that will live in infamy. Elvis has left the building."

Gabe was such a smart ass. They were doing this for him as well as for Twenties Girl, who had yet to make an appearance, yet he was making jokes. Not a surprise, really. Gabe may have won her trust on some level but Natalie and Liam were strangers to her.

Liam's frown deepened before he glanced up at Natalie again. "Nothing."

"Well, maybe one of them is here and talking and your device just isn't picking it up," she said, hoping he got the message that the breakdown wasn't on Gabe's end. She turned to her friend. "Harper? Anything?"

She shook her head. "No. I don't know if I'm happy or not about that. It would be reassuring if someone else could hear them too."

Natalie could relate to that.

"But I never heard anything down here," Harper continued. "It's always upstairs in the attic."

"I had wondered if it might be the exact location that enables you to hear him—uh, them." Liam corrected quickly.

Ha! Maybe now he would understand how hard it was to not slip up and stop judging her for how often she did.

"Can we go upstairs and try?" Natalie asked after enjoying her victory for a moment.

"Of course," Harper answered and turned for the

stairs. "Anything to help. Agnes wasn't too keen on the exorcism idea but said she'd allow it if it would make me happy. Stone just shook his head and walked away. So I'm open to any solutions before I become a complete outcast around here."

After a backward glance to make sure Gabe was following the procession, Natalie kept her eyes peeled for the girl ghost, without luck.

Finally they were in the attic, accessible by a back staircase.

The top floor was as long as the house and had amazingly high vaulted ceilings and big windows at each end. It was nothing like the low unfinished attic with the pull-down ladder in the ranch style house where Natalie had grown up.

The space was amazing on its own, but even more so since it had been renovated to be a kind of apartment for Harper. She could have used any one of the many bedrooms on the second floor of Agnes's house but given that Stone had pretty much moved in to be with Harper, Natalie supposed they wanted the privacy that having a whole floor to themselves afforded.

To themselves *except* for Gabe and Twenties Girl... and Natalie really did have to ask him if he'd gotten her name.

Another glance around the space told Natalie the resident spirit was still hiding. At least from her view.

"Harper, you said there were noises in the closets. Maybe we should try taking some readings in there?" Natalie suggested.

Not that she had any idea what kind of readings Liam was taking, but she did want to see if the ghost was hiding in the closet.

"Sure. Go ahead. Watch out. The one is packed full of Agnes's stuff. The other one is pretty organized though— I had a book deadline recently so I cleaned the closet," Harper explained in a statement that only a good friend of hers who knew her tendency toward chronic procrastination would understand.

Liam looked a tad confused but headed for the first storage room—the one used by Agnes for storage— and repeated his prompt, asking for any ghosts to make their presence known.

Again Gabe spoke. When Liam shook his head Gabe went so far as to stomp his feet on the floor. Then he tried to knock over a roll of wrapping paper. Still nothing.

"I don't know." Gabe shrugged.

"Is it the time of day possibly?" Natalie asked. She turned to Harper. "When exactly have you been hearing things?"

"The second time was late. Like the middle of the night. I was asleep in bed and it woke me up. But the first time was early. I'd gone upstairs right after the LADS meeting at your shop to get some work done. Then I heard it."

"So not dependent on midnight or full dark then. Hmm." Liam looked pensively perplexed.

Natalie on the other hand was starting to panic.

She didn't know what she expected him to find or how it would help but maybe if Harper heard Gabe with them around she'd calm down. Or if Harper could hear him clearly say he meant her no harm, maybe she'd call off the exorcism. But if they couldn't recreate what had happened before—couldn't get her to hear him again, or at all—Twenties Girl and possibly countless other ghosts were screwed.

"What now?" Natalie asked Liam.

He bobbed his head to one side. "I can take some EMF readings in the basement while I'm here. See if this has anything to do with electromagnetic fields."

Natalie cringed. Gabe didn't look too happy either at the mention of the creepy basement.

Liam continued, "Besides that, I can leave a voice activated recorder in the closet where you heard them and see if we catch anything over night."

Harper nodded. "Okay. That's fine. I'm not

sleeping up here anyway until this is resolved. I convinced Stone to temporarily move to a bedroom on the second floor."

"The one with the balcony and the connecting bathroom with the clawfoot tub?" Natalie asked, knowing it was Harper's favorite room in the house.

It was also the room with the ominous numbers scratched into the woodwork where she'd first found Twenties Girl hiding.

When Harper nodded, Natalie had nothing else to say except, "Oh. That's good."

While they'd been talking, Liam had set his ghost trap—that being the voice activated recorder—in the closet. That could be of use to her actually. She hadn't given up on convincing Harper Gabe meant no harm.

If Gabe spoke into the machine and told Harper he was friendly, apologized for scaring her and promised to stay away—and then actually did stay away—maybe she'd forget about the exorcism and start sleeping in her own room again.

It was worth a try.

Liam preceded them downstairs to go down to the basement, where Natalie had no intention of following. Behind him, Harper and Natalie made their way downstairs more slowly.

She noticed Gabe wasn't behind them.

He was probably searching for the girl. Good. He could explain to her what was happening. She had a right to know. She was probably frightened after having all these people and strange equipment invading her space. The poor thing.

"I'm sorry we couldn't catch anything," Natalie said when they reached the first floor.

Harper shrugged. "It's okay. After Agnes agreed—however reluctantly—I was able to get on the exorcist's calendar. She has an opening this week."

"This week. So soon?" Natalie asked, panicked.

Harper nodded. "I was lucky."

"Yeah. Lucky," Natalie agreed.

And so the countdown began…

Chapter Fourteen

Sitting on the tattered old sofa in the shop's meeting room, Natalie leaned forward and looked to each of the men opposite her. Liam sitting in the chair and Gabe standing next to him.

"I don't think we have anything to worry about," she began.

Liam nodded. "I agree."

At the same time, Gabe snorted. "Easy for you to say. In just a few hours I could be dissolved into the ether and cease to exist completely."

Harper had dropped off the voice recorder from the attic and Liam had confirmed it hadn't captured any voices even though Gabe insisted he'd spoken into it, assuring Harper he was a friendly ghost.

That meant Harper was going ahead with the exorcism *tonight*.

Natalie directed her gaze to Gabe. "Hear me out. I did a lot of research since leaving Harper's after our little ghost hunt and here's what I learned about this exorcism she has planned..."

Gabe scowled. "Do tell. I can't wait to hear."

Ignoring Gabe's sarcasm, Natalie continued, "An actual real exorcism has to be performed by an official priest. I got Harper to tell me who she hired and it looks like just some woman who sells her 'house cleansing' services."

Liam raised his hand as if this were a class and he was a student. "Actually, I did a bit of research myself and though it is true an ordained official has to perform the highest level of exorcism—such as possession of a person—there's an appendix to the rites to address places and objects. And those rites can be administered by a lay person. But here's the thing, almost everything I read refers to demons. Demonic possession, demonic infestation."

"Gabe's not a demon," Natalie said.

"Exactly. So suspending my doubt that exorcism works at all, and assuming it does, would it even work on a spirit that's not demonic?" Liam, ever the researcher, asked.

"I bet he didn't believe in ghosts either until you and me," Gabe said directly to Natalie. "So forgive me if I'm not comforted by his doubts about exorcism now."

Pressing her lips together, Natalie ignored Gabe's snide remarks and tried to sort out their next course of action. "Okay. I think the safest thing to do is plan for the worst-case scenario."

"That being what?" Liam asked.

"That this woman isn't a fraud and the invocations or whatever in this appendix you mention can work and that they can work on all spirits not just the malevolent."

Liam cocked up a brow. "Those are a whole lot of assumptions."

"Yes. But better to be prepared than not. So assuming all of that I think the safest thing to do is get any and all ghosts far away from Agnes's house tonight during the ritual." Natalie turned her focus to Gabe. "Including Twenties Girl. Can you do that? Convince her to leave?"

"I think so. I'm going to have to or..." He visibly swallowed.

"It's going to be okay. Like Liam said, we're making a lot of assumptions that this can even work. But if it does, the range can't reach out into the community. There has to be a limit, geographically speaking."

Gabe nodded. "Okay. I'm going to the cemetery to ask Ricky to spread the word to everyone in town, then I'll go convince Millie."

"Millie?" Natalie asked.

Gabe tipped his head. "Twenties Girl."

"I didn't know you'd learned her name. That's nice. I'm glad."

He rolled his eyes. "I'm so glad you're happy. Can I go now? I have like an hour to try and save the entire ghost population of Mudville."

"Yes. Go."

Without even a goodbye, Gabe swooped through the wall.

"He gone?" Liam asked.

Natalie sighed. This whole thing had been exhausting. "Yes."

"Would you like to catch me up on the conversation?" Liam asked.

She frowned as she tried to remember what they'd even talked about, specifically.

"Millie?" Liam prompted.

"Oh. Yeah. That's the nineteen-twenties ghost hanging out at Harper's house. The one that Gabe was visiting the two times that Harper heard them."

"Visiting, huh?" Liam smirked.

"What's that supposed to mean?" she asked.

"What's this Millie look like? She cute?"

Natalie frowned. "What do you care if she's cute or not?"

"Jeezus, Nat. I'm not asking for me. As if I'd be able to see or hear her anyway?" Liam shook his head. "I'm asking because I'm thinking Gabe might have a little ghost crush on this Millie."

"You think?" She considered that.

The girl was lovely. Young. At least young to Natalie's forty-year-old eyes, but not a child. She was definitely old enough to date. Although, Gabe was probably double her age. Not that it mattered. There was a long-standing tradition of men dating women half their age. Both parties being dead didn't change that, she supposed.

"You're awfully quiet." Liam's brow cocked up high. "I seriously hope it's not that you're jealous over the fact Gabe has a new interest in someone else besides you."

Natalie rolled her eyes. "Stop. It's never been like that between me and Gabe. You know that."

"Even so. He spends like half his time with you. How are you going to feel if he gets a new bestie?" Liam asked.

"I'll feel relieved that I'll have more time to spend with my boyfriend, if he ever stops acting like an ass." She crossed her arms to glare at him, even though in the back of her mind was a niggling thought that what Liam said might be true.

Gabe had become a fixture in her life. What would she feel if that changed? If he wasn't around anymore. Not just because he could become busy with Millie, but worse, because this damn house cleansing might just work.

Natalie stood. "I have to close up and get ready to go to Harper's."

"You're going?" Liam asked, standing as well.

"Harper said I could be there. I think I'll feel better being on site, you know? Just in case." She fought the sick feeling in the pit of her stomach. "Any chance you want to come?"

"Because Gabe can't?" Liam asked with that damn cocky brow raised again.

Feeling vulnerable, she said, "No. Because I'm a little scared and I want you with me."

Liam took a step forward and pulled her into his arms. "In that case, yeah, I'll come. I'll always be there for you when you need me."

"Thank you."

Now if only she could be sure Gabe and all the rest

of the ghosts she'd complained about over the past year would always be there for her too. She'd gotten used to them being around town. As used as she was to seeing Alice or Mary or Agnes and the rest of the livings.

It was completely true. A person didn't miss something—or someone—until it was gone.

Chapter Fifteen

AN HOUR OR SO LATER, LIAM PAUSED AT THE bottom step of the staircase that led to the front porch of Agnes's house and glanced up—way up—at the ornate facade of the yellow Victorian. "This really is a nice house."

Any other day, Natalie would have launched into tour guide mode, delivering the history of the house and pointing out architectural details and all the things she'd learned since meeting Harper. All the things they hadn't discussed the other day when they'd been there and Liam had been in ghost hunter mode.

Today, all she managed to say was, "Yeah, it is," as she continued to climb the steps ahead of him.

She wouldn't say she was afraid, but she certainly wasn't completely confident.

At this point all she could do was hope for a positive outcome. Hope that Gabe had successfully cleared this end of the village of all the ghosts—including Millie who was the one in the most danger.

The warmth of Liam's hand on the back of her neck was a small comfort as she reached for the doorbell. Nerves riding her, she used the knocker too, just to make sure Harper heard her.

"It'll be fine," Liam said.

"It had better be," she mumbled as Harper unlocked the door and pulled it wide.

"Hi," Harper greeted as her gaze went from Natalie to Liam.

"Is it okay we're here?" Natalie asked.

"Of course. Agnes and Stone are both here too. Come on in." Harper led them inside. "Stone's in the kitchen and the preparations for the rites are happening in the dining room."

As they made their way through the center hall, she said to Liam, "You can go join Stone in the kitchen if you want."

Natalie tried to sound lighter than she felt. She didn't know if she succeeded.

"Yes, please do," Harper said. "He'll be happy to have another man to grumble about all this woo-woo mumbo-jumbo to. I'll show you the way."

With one last concerned glance at Natalie, Liam nodded and followed Harper through to the kitchen while Natalie took the opportunity to look around.

She didn't see Millie or Gabe. Or hear them.

Sadly she'd never been able to feel the spirits. Never could sense when they were near. It was just like they were people—living people that is. If they were in front of her she could see them. If not, she couldn't. What she'd give to be able to sense their presence just to be sure there weren't any here now.

She'd have to trust in Gabe. That he'd done what he said he would—

While Harper was getting Liam settled with Stone in the kitchen, Natalie wandered into the living room where she had a clear view straight into the dining room.

There she was. The layman exorcist. The house cleanser.

Younger than Natalie expected—although she hadn't been sure what to expect—the woman was dressed in a long sweeping skirt in a deep purple. The hem came to the tops of her feet, which were—at the moment—completely bare. A loose, shapeless tunic in a bright, intricate patchwork pattern flowed over the skirt.

Her hair was long and blonde with the tips dyed purple.

As she arranged items on the dining room table the multitude of metal bracelets she wore on each wrist clanked together in an almost musical accompaniment to her movements.

Was she a charlatan? Or a legitimate medium.

Natalie was so engrossed watching, so deep in her own mind as she struggled to form an opinion about this woman, she was startled when the medium's gaze locked on hers.

"Hello. Are you here for the cleansing?"

"Uh, yes. If that's okay."

"Of course. You're not sensitive to smoke, are you?" The young blonde lifted what Natalie recognized as a sage wand from all the many times the Wiccans had come in to cleanse her shop of negative energy—

A thought struck her.

The Wiccans had smudged her shop with Gabe standing in it and he'd been fine. Maybe this was going to be okay.

Immensely relieved, she hoped not prematurely, Natalie realized the woman was waiting for an answer. "No. I actually like the smell of the sage. Thanks for asking."

She smiled. "Of course. And I like the smell of it too," she said conspiratorially. "I might be guilty of using it at home way more often than necessary."

Real or fake, the woman was charming and Natalie was beginning to like her in spite of herself.

"How long have you been doing this—cleansing houses?" Natalie asked.

The blonde laughed. "Oh, no. It's not me. I'm Jill. I'm just an assistant. An intern on a spiritual journey to enlightenment. I'm not sure I'll ever be as talented as Madame Letisha—she's the medium and my mystic mentor. She'll be here any moment. I lay out her things and handle any mundane earthly matters like the business of payment. She's above all that. She must be in order for her to be able to completely commune on the spiritual plane. She's very good."

Natalie listened with eyebrows raised.

Her first thought was to wish that Liam was in the room to hear this, just so he could confirm it was indeed as big a load of manure as she thought it was.

Her second thought was to wish Gabe were here too. He'd be doubled over laughing.

But her third thought had her pausing. What if Madame Letisha—as over the top as she seemed— actually did have some power?

If someone had told Natalie a year ago that she'd

be talking to ghosts, she'd have laughed them out of the room. But here she was, a conduit to the entire ghostly world. And to believe she was the only one on earth with that power would be hubris in the extreme.

Agnes, Liam, Harper and Stone had appeared in the doorway while Natalie was having her unwelcome revelation.

Liam took one look at her expression and came forward. Leaning low, he pressed a kiss to her cheek and then said against her ear, "Everything all right?"

She lifted her face to look at him and said low, "I guess we're going to see."

Chapter Sixteen

"Quiet! I must concentrate."

Natalie's eyes opened wide at the censure that she'd earned simply by the poorly timed vibration of the cell phone in her pocket.

Madame Letisha had indeed arrived and she was a piece of work.

The woman's larger than life personality was a match for her appearance.

She had a wild mass of jet-black curls highlighted with strands of gray and lips painted a bright red. Her over the top style of dress—from the brightly colored head wrap to the bells on her shoes—made her assistant Jill's outfit seem staid by comparison.

Natalie cringed as she caught Harper's eye and mouthed, "Sorry."

Harper waved away her concern as Natalie rushed to pull the phone out. Ignoring the text from Jules, she mashed the button on the side to power the cell down before it offended Madame Letisha again and got her thrown out of the performance.

And this clearly was a performance.

A show to impress them all, but in particular Harper, who was footing the bill. Natalie was sure this wasn't cheap judging by Madame Letisha's appearance.

The jewels dripping off her every finger, wrists and neck, not to mention the Mercedes she'd pulled up in told Natalie this must be a lucrative gig.

If Once Upon a Vine were to fail, she supposed she could always become a professional medium to survive.

But Madame Letisha was so much more than a medium. She was a showman. Worthy of vaudeville. Or maybe a carnival.

Yes, that was it. Madame Letisha could easily be a carny. Traveling the country with the rest of the troop as a headliner. The top money maker.

There was no question she was talented as an actor. The question was, did she actually have any abilities?

"First I will cleanse the space," Madame Letisha announced.

She raised the sage wand high in the air and mumbled some words Natalie didn't understand. Neither did the others in the room if their expressions were any indication.

Liam was barely containing a smile. Stone, jaw set, looked ready to toss the woman out the front door. Agnes watched with tempered skepticism. And Harper still managed to maintain a look that was hopeful although a bit of doubt crept onto her continence.

Natalie could almost read the thoughts going through her friend's mind as a *what did I get myself into* expression crossed Harper's face.

The smudging took an inordinately long time.

Madame Letisha fluttered around the large house directing the sage smoke into every corner and then out an open window. She gave each room on the first floor the same treatment, before leading them up the stairs to perform the same ritual on the second and then the third floor.

Upstairs Natalie did less watching of the show as she concentrated on keeping an eye out for Millie. She'd hadn't heard from Gabe again. She didn't know if he'd convinced Millie to leave. She hoped he had, even if Madame Letisha's skills were severely in doubt at the moment. At least as far as Natalie was concerned.

"Now I will determine if the cleansing was successful."

Standing in the middle of Harper's attic bedroom, Madame Letisha thrust out one arm ramrod straight. That spurred her assistant into action. The blonde sprang forward and after what could only be described as a bow, she laid a multicolored pendulum in her mentor's palm.

"This pendulum is used for divination." Letisha delivered that in a tone so serious there was no doubt she believed the wisdom she imparted was the most important thing they'd all hear all day.

As Natalie wished she could secretly record this performance on her phone to share with Jules and Gabe later, the medium held one arm straight out and stilled the motion of the pendulum with her other hand.

"I will now communicate with the pendulum. I respectfully ask that you indicate the motion you will use for the word 'No'."

The pendulum began to move, a small, barely perceptible movement at first, then larger until it was swinging visibly in a wide circle.

Liam leaned down. "Is she moving it?"

"Silence!"

After that censure, Natalie didn't dare answer him.

Pressing his lips tight, Liam straightened to his full height and remained silent as they all, equally as quiet, watched as Madame Letisha thanked the pendulum.

Then she said, "I respectfully request you show me the motion to indicate the word 'Yes'."

The pendulum again complied and began to swing from side to side.

"We understand your motion for the answers of Yes and No. I will now ask you the questions we desire answers to."

Natalie couldn't wait to hear these.

"Are there any spirits living in this house?"

The pendulum began to swing from side to side.

"The answer is yes."

Of course the madame would want the pendulum to say yes, or there would be no reason for Harper to pay her to be here.

What was confusing was the phrasing of the question. Millie lived in the house, yes. But she wasn't there right now—hopefully—so if the question were phrased slightly different the answer would have been different as well.

As it stood, Natalie couldn't determine if Madame

Letisha and her pendulum were all knowing and powerful, or not.

Feeling brave—perhaps foolishly—Natalie raised her hand. "Um, can I ask it a question?"

"No!"

Natalie regrouped. "Then can I suggest a question for you to ask?"

If Madame Letisha weren't so deep into character, Natalie's persistence might have thrown her off her game, but as it was, the woman remained stalwart. "Go on."

Victorious, Natalie said, "Ask it if there are any spirits in the house at this very moment."

That did earn her a raised eyebrow, but Madame Letisha repeated the question verbatim. The pendulum began swinging from side to side.

"The answer is again yes," Madame Letisha delivered with a glare at Natalie.

"Thank you," Natalie said, although even that question hadn't been very helpful either in determining Madame Letisha or the pendulum's accuracy.

Natalie hadn't seen Millie but that didn't mean the girl wasn't there hiding. And Madame Letisha, fake or real, still had a fifty-fifty chance of being right either way.

"I cannot say that you are welcome," Madam Letisha delivered with a glare. "Now please, no more interruptions."

Wincing, Natalie said, "Sorry."

"I respectfully ask is there more than one spirit living in this home?"

The answer was once again yes.

"Are there more than two?"

Yes again.

"More than three?"

At that question and the resulting predictable answer of yes, Harper gasped while Stone scoffed and shook his head.

Natalie caught Liam's gaze.

She'd explained to him the ghosts' aversion to funeral homes and how that's why it was so surprising they'd found Millie there. There was no way three or more spirits were living in this house. And if by some stretch of the imagination there were, Gabe would have seen them when he was here trying to get Millie to talk and reported back on it.

Liam knew as well as she did that either Madame Letisha or her pendulum was lying.

"Did the cleansing ritual I performed rid this home of the spirits residing here?"

The pendulum began to spin in a circle.

"The answer is no." Madame Letisha thrust her arm out straight, spurring her intern into action once again as Jill trotted forward and took the pendulum.

"We must take further steps to cleanse this home. I will speak directly to the spirits. Should they be agreeable, I will convince them to move elsewhere."

Harper nodded and the woman raised her face and gazed upward.

Natalie tipped her head back and looked up as well, impressed when she saw what a nice job Stone had done on the vaulted ceiling when he'd converted the attic from storage into living space.

Meanwhile, Madame Letisha began to hum, a low tuneless drone that built from soft to loud.

Natalie caught Liam's eye but had to look away or risk laughing when she saw him biting his lip to hold in a smile.

Then Madame Letisha went completely and suddenly silent before she began to speak. "Spirits! Hear me now. You are not welcome in this space. With open hearts and joyful minds, we wish you peace and light but you must move on."

She stopped and appeared to listen, as if she could hear them and their reply. Even going so far as to cup her ear to hear better.

"They have agreed to move on," she announced.

Harper drew back. "Really? Are you sure?"

Madame Letisha turned back to the non-existent spirits. "Should any lingering energy reside in this space, do not remain here. We bid you find solace and release. Return to where you truly belong."

With two sharp claps, she bowed her head and closed her eyes, and then Madame Letisha breathed in a loud breath, the volume of which was only surpassed by her even louder exhale.

She raised her head, saying, "They are gone."

With a dramatic swoosh of her skirt, the woman turned toward Harper.

"I have created for you a safe haven where positive energy thrives. From this day forward there will be love and laughter in this home."

Now it was Agnes's turn to scoff as she mumbled, "There always has been."

Perhaps it was Agnes's age or the fact she was the homeowner, but the comment didn't earn her any censure.

Instead, Madame Letisha said, "I am drained. I must leave and go rest. My assistant will collect payment."

Then with a jangle of jewelry and another swoosh of fabric, she whooshed out of the room, followed closely by Jill at her heels.

Once they were gone, Natalie was free to bury her face in Liam's chest, partly to smother the laugh she'd been holding in but mostly with relief.

Madame Letisha was full of bullshit. Natalie truly believed that now.

But she wouldn't feel completely calm until she laid eyes on Gabe.

Chapter Seventeen

"WELL, THAT'S THAT THEN," AGNES SAID, following the two women who'd preceded her down the stairs.

"Yup." Harper drew in a breath and let it out as she glanced at those remaining in the room. She turned her focus on Natalie. "I just have to pay her, then we can hang out if you want."

The fear that by some strange twist of fate Madame Letisha's ceremony had actually worked rubbed against Natalie's nerves like sandpaper.

Were they all okay?

The question would continue to chafe until she saw for herself. She wouldn't be able to hide her distraction from Harper, nor would she enjoy the time spent here when she desperately needed to be elsewhere.

She couldn't wait to confirm Gabe and the others were safe, so she had to come up with an excuse on the fly. "Um, thanks, but I left a pile of work back at the shop I need to do tonight. Thank you so much for letting us come. It was... interesting."

"That's one word for it," Stone mumbled as he headed down the stairs with Harper. Natalie and Liam followed.

When they reached the first floor, Natalie still hadn't seen any signs of ghosts. But that was to be expected. Right? She'd told Gabe to clear the house. The real test would be once she left here and got back to the other end of town.

Liam glanced down at Natalie with one comforting hand pressed against her lower back. "Ready to go?"

"Yes, please."

They said a quick goodbye and another thanks to Harper before she had to skitter off to pay and then finally, Natalie was free to head outside and start her search.

"So what do you think? Bullshit, right?" Liam asked.

"I can't be sure until I see them," she answered,

becoming short of breath as they strode fast down the sidewalk toward the train depot.

Usually when they walked side-by-side Liam had to slow his much longer stride to accommodate Natalie's shorter legs. This time, she led the way and it was up to him to match his speed to her faster one.

She couldn't get back to the shop fast enough. With any luck Gabe would be there with some of the others, taking shelter. Waiting out the storm, so to speak.

Her hand shook as she tried to get the key into the lock.

Liam obviously noticed. Once again Natalie found comfort in his big warm hand, this time as he gave a small squeeze on her shoulder.

"It's going to be okay," he said.

Drawing in a breath as she turned the key in the lock, she glanced up and said, "I hope so." Then she opened the door.

The shop appeared empty. But that didn't mean he wasn't in the meeting room or back in her apartment.

"Gabe?" she called. Walking farther inside she called his name again.

Nothing. She rushed to the back window and looked out.

Not even train track dude was out walking the tracks.

She spun to Liam, "No one's here."

"Maybe they're in the lab?" he suggested.

"Yes. Good idea. Let's go check." She wrestled with the lock on the back door.

Flinging it open, she rushed out into the night air leaving Liam to secure the door behind her.

She literally ran to the warehouse—and running was not something Natalie did unless absolutely necessary.

When she arrived, slightly ahead of Liam, she banged on the door and called out, "Gabe! Are you in there?"

Liam caught up quickly and punched in the key code to unlock the door. He opened it and allowed her to enter first.

"Gabe?"

Again, nothing. She spun to Liam.

"He's not here. And I don't even see Ethel or Myra." And as far as she knew, they were total homebodies and never left the warehouse. At Liam's frown, she elaborated. "The two old lady cadavers."

He punched in the code to disable the alarm and turned to her. "Oh. They were picked up. Although I have to say it's a relief to know their spirits left with their bodies and didn't hang around."

Natalie let out a breath. "Okay. That makes sense. Gabe doesn't like hanging out here with his decapitated body."

Liam barely controlled an eye roll. "I know. I've said I'm sorry."

She waved away his concern. "It's more likely they're somewhere they all usually hang out anyway. Like the cemetery."

"Then let's go."

"You don't mind?" she asked. Dragging Liam all over town looking for ghosts seemed like a lot to ask.

He shook his head. "Nope. But we're driving. Okay?"

It wasn't that far but she wasn't going to argue. "Okay."

Liam grabbed his keys off the desk and followed her outside.

The whole quarter of a mile that she sat in the passenger seat she strained to look for someone, anyone, from the spirit realm.

"Anything?" Liam asked.

"No. Ooo. Wait. Slow down!"

Liam hit the brakes and for one brief blissful moment

she thought she saw a ghost in front of the pharmacy, but when he reached out and swung the door open she realized it was just a man. Old, yes, but still living.

She slumped back against the seat. "Never mind. False alarm. Sorry."

"It's fine. We're close enough to the cemetery I'm just gonna park."

Hope restored, she leaned forward again and waited for the vehicle to finally come to a stop before she flung open the door and then remembered to unbuckle her seat belt.

Running across the sidewalk, she gripped the elaborate iron fence and scanned the area.

"Gabe!" she whisper-yelled. "Is there anybody here?"

It wasn't late and there were people around. She couldn't outright shout into the historic cemetery. And she couldn't go walking through it either since it was after dusk and technically closed for visitors.

But it probably didn't matter because she should have seen someone by now. If anyone were there, she'd have seen them already.

Liam joined her against the fence. "Anything?"

"No," she said thickly through the tightness in her throat. "Any chance you think they would all squish into that one mausoleum over there?"

"How many are there?" he asked.

"Close to a hundred, I guess. Definitely more than fifty." At his silence she glanced up and found Liam staring at her, his mouth open.

"That many?"

"Yeah."

Finally he swallowed. "Then no. I doubt they'd fit." He drew in a breath and blew it out. "Anywhere else you can think they might be?"

She turned to face Liam fully. "I have seen them at the bar."

Liam's eyes flicked wide before he ran one hand over his stubble. "The bar too?"

"Baby, I hate to tell you this, but they're everywhere."

Or at least they used to be. That sick feeling renewed itself in her gut.

"Can we check the bar?" she asked.

"No problem. I could use a drink after this."

She could too.

Loaded back in Liam's Jeep they traveled the half a mile more to the local bar. Liam parked while Natalie scanned the scenery. There were lots of locals, but all of the living variety as far as she could tell.

Inside, she swept her gaze from the bar to the pool table and then the seating area.

"Anything?" Liam asked leaning low to be heard over the juke box.

She shook her head.

"You wanna leave and go check somewhere else?"

Fighting tears, she said, "No. Let's stay and have something to eat."

"You sure?" he asked.

They'd never gotten to eat before going to Harper's. Her stomach might be churning with worry, but Liam had to be hungry.

She nodded. "Yeah. We'll eat and then head home."

"Okay. If you're sure," he said.

"I am. They're probably just afraid to come out tonight. I'm sure I'll see them in the morning."

She could only hope she was right.

Chapter Eighteen

A GHOST-FREE NIGHT WITH LIAM WAS ALL Natalie had wished for on many occasions, but now that she had one she couldn't even enjoy it. Not while crippled with worry like she was.

Liam was a doll. Of course it was possible he was simply happy that Gabe—his biggest rival for her attention aside from the shop—might be gone for good.

But he assured her he would stay with her at her apartment all night. He made her tea and put on a movie he knew she would like. He wrapped her in a blanket on the sofa and held her until she felt warm and safe—but still no less worried.

No amount of tea or chick flicks would be able to

distract her from her fear that she'd seen her last Mudville ghost.

Strange how she could miss so keenly the very thing that she'd so often viewed as a problem.

Liam hugged her tighter and pressed a kiss to the top of her head. "You doing okay?"

No.

"Yes."

"Do you want me to—" Liam stopped mid-sentence.

Frowning, he eased away from her.

"Did you hear that?" he asked, his voice low.

"Hear what—"

"Shh!" Snapping into warrior mode, Liam launched off the sofa and mouthed, "Voices. You stay here."

To hell with that.

If there was an intruder inside her shop, she had every intention of confronting them. She'd do it while standing safely behind her big scary former-military boyfriend but still, she wasn't going to hide in her apartment alone while he went out there.

Natalie stood. She tiptoed behind Liam into the darkened shop lit only by the shaft of moonlight streaming inside. It illuminated the front table with the new releases on it but not much more.

It certainly wasn't enough for her to see any burglars or vandals who might be hiding amid the shelves.

She reached for the light switch and found Liam's hand already there. He flipped the switch, flooding the shop with light, then he paused, listening. "There. Again. A man's voice—"

Natalie stopped listening to Liam when Gabe came into view and said her name.

"Oh my God. You're alive! Uh, I mean—you know what I mean." Teary-eyed, she rushed forward then stopped. "I'd hug you if I could."

He smiled. "Missed me, did you?"

"I thought you were gone. Everyone. I looked everywhere. I couldn't find even one of you. Not even train track dude."

"We're all in that really nice, big old house up on the hill. You know the one with the stone columns along the road and the long driveway?"

She shook her head. She didn't know the house, but she didn't care. Gabe was all right. They all were.

"Everyone else is still there but I wanted to come down and get an update on the exorcism. What happened at Harper's?"

Breathing in, Natalie tried to slow her speeding

heart. Everything was fine, her head knew that but it was taking her body a little while to catch up.

"It was ridiculous. I wish you had been there. This woman has to be a complete charlatan and I'm glad if she is because that means you were never in any danger. And Millie too. I didn't see her over there. Did you get her out?"

"Yeah, actually, about that." Gabe glanced behind a bookcase and extended one hand. "Come on. It's okay."

At that urging, the ghost formerly known as Twenties Girl came into view.

Gabe took her hand in his and said, "Natalie, I'd like to officially introduce you to Millie. Millie, this is my friend Natalie, the living who can see us."

"Pleasure to meet you," Millie said, so shyly Natalie barely heard her.

Liam clamped one big hand so tightly onto Natalie's shoulder she said, "Ow."

"Nat," he said, his voice sounding strange.

"Yeah?" She covered his hand with hers and began to pry his fingers off her before he left bruises.

When she twisted enough to see his face she saw something she'd never seen before. Not even when they'd been tied up by a murderer. Fear.

"I heard that. Him. Gabe. And her. I hear them."

"What?" She turned from Liam to Gabe. "How is that possible?"

He shrugged. "I have no idea."

"*I have no idea*," Liam repeated Gabe's words verbatim. "That's what he just said."

What was happening?

Gabe dropped his hold on Millie's hand and took a step forward.

"Can you see me too?" he asked Liam directly.

When he received no reaction at all, not even a blink from Liam, Gabe turned to Natalie. "Am I going in and out, like a shoddy cell signal?"

"I don't know."

Liam turned to Natalie. "I don't hear him anymore."

"I know. We're trying to figure out why," she told him while Gabe reached back and took Millie's hand again.

"You all right?" Gabe asked the girl.

It sounded so much like what Liam had said to Natalie so many times tonight while she'd been upset, that she realized what Liam had suggested might be true. Gabe liked Millie. Liked her as more than a friend.

"He just asked, *are you all right*," Liam said, his eyes wide again.

"He heard that?" Gabe asked.

"I heard that," Liam answered.

"What is going on?" Natalie asked, looking from one man to the other.

Millie took a single step forward then lifted her and Gabe's entwined hands. Looking at Gabe, she said, "It's when you're holding my hand."

Gabe frowned then glanced at Natalie. "I think she's right. Do you hear me now?"

"Yes, and I heard her," Liam answered. "Jeezus, this is nuts."

"Wait." Gabe dropped Millie's hand. "How about now? Liam? Hello, Liam."

They all turned to see Liam waiting patiently.

Gabe took Millie's hand again. "Liam?"

Liam sucked in a breath. "Yes, Gabe."

"That's what it is. He can hear us whenever I'm touching Millie. And it must have worked for Harper too. I had grabbed Millie before I knocked over the tree and she ran away."

Natalie moved the sign that read *New Releases* closer to Gabe and said, "Hold her hand and knock that over."

He didn't question her but poked at the sign. It tipped over onto the table.

Liam's eyes got impossibly wider. "Ho-ly shit."

Gabe spun back to Liam. "But you still *can't* see us?"

"Correct," Liam confirmed.

"I still don't understand. Why do we think this is happening?" Gabe asked as he pulled Millie closer to him and gazed down at her face.

"I think I might know." Natalie couldn't help the small, sad smile that bowed her lips.

Things were about to change, and that included her and Gabe's friendship because it was obvious to her that her best friend was in love.

Chapter Nineteen

Natalie shot Liam a glance across the small table in what served as a kitchen area in her apartment. "You all right?"

A mug filled with his first coffee of the morning clutched in one big hand, he said, "Why wouldn't I be?"

"You just heard your first ghost last night."

"You hear *and* see them all the time and you're okay," he pointed out.

"Now I am. At the beginning, not so much."

She remembered the first day when she realized she could see and hear members of the spirit realm. She'd wondered if she needed to see a neurologist or possibly a psychotherapist.

But unlike her, Liam wasn't alone in his

experience. He had Natalie there as a spiritual guide, so to speak. And he'd already known of Gabe's existence before being able to actually speak with him.

That they could speak now still blew her mind. It was as amazing as it was concerning. Hopefully Gabe would keep all of his many snide comments to himself now that Liam might be able to hear them.

And it was all because of Millie... Amazing.

Love was a powerful thing. This seemed like indisputable proof of that.

"I'll be fine. How are you?" Liam asked, turning the question back on her.

"I'm good. Why?"

"Well, you have to share your bestie now."

Denying the truth of her concern, she waved his comment away. "I'm sure he'll still be hanging around here too often for my liking, in spite of his relationship with Millie."

"Hmm. Interesting."

She frowned at Liam. "What's interesting?"

"I was talking about how you'll feel sharing Gabe with *me* now that I can talk to him myself directly instead of going through you as an interpreter. Yet you jumped right to the fact that you'll have to share him with his girlfriend."

Natalie rolled her eyes. "I'm not interested in Gabe romantically."

Liam bobbed his head. "Maybe not."

"I'm not!"

"Okay, you're not. But you're still used to him being at your beck and call."

She shook her head and frowned. "No."

"Yes," Liam countered. "When I wouldn't go to that meeting with you, Gabe did. When I'm busy working, he keeps you company in the shop. When you want to discuss ghost stuff, he's your go to. Maybe he won't be so accessible to you now he's in a relationship."

She scowled. "You're being silly. Harper's engaged and I still see her all the time." Not even close to half as much as she saw—or used to see—Gabe, but...

"We'll see." Liam shrugged. "So what's next?"

"What's next for what?" she asked grateful for the subject change.

"For you. For the ghosts. Whatever. Now that Harper's appeased her house is 'clean', the ghosts are all safe from Madame Letisha, and I can hear Gabe without you being the go between, there's nothing more for you to worry about. Whatever will you do with all your time, Ms. Chase?" he asked with a smirk.

"Well, smart ass. Besides my full-time job running

the shop, there's still the mystery of the backyard bone to worry about."

Not to mention the holes from the search crew that her insurance company would no doubt consider a liability.

"And I would love to interview Millie and learn what her story is. I never got around to telling you, but Gabe heard a rumor in the graveyard—"

"Is that where all the good ghost goss comes from. The graveyard?" Liam laughed.

"The *ghost goss*? And yes, it is. Shh. I'm telling a story."

"Sorry."

"I forgive you. Anyway, he heard there were rumors that someone was killed in Agnes's house and they never found the body. I'm thinking it has to be Millie. And what if the reason they never found the body is because it was buried behind the train depot?"

Liam tipped his head. "A few leaps there but I guess anything is possible."

"The question is, how did she die?" she asked.

"The ghost rumor mill didn't supply that?"

"Not that Gabe said. And he said he hasn't been able to get her to talk about it. You haven't seen her but she's young and beautiful. She looks completely healthy. I mean there's no visible sign of what killed her. I'm kind of intrigued."

Liam grunted. "Hmm. And now so am I. Intrigued. All right, Nancy Drew. Then let's plan it. Invite Gabe and Millie over."

"Like a double date?"

He laughed. "Well, no. I was thinking more like for a chat but call it whatever you want."

"Okay. I'll ask next time he comes into the shop. If he's not too busy and has time to stop by."

"Jealousy..." Liam sang.

She stuck her tongue out at him. "If that isn't the pot calling the kettle black."

Liam laughed. "So I'm not broken up that my girlfriend's ghost boyfriend got himself a ghost girlfriend. Sue me."

Chapter Twenty

NATALIE GLANCED AT THE CLOCK FOR WHAT had to be the tenth time in the past few hours. Was the day moving extra slowly today? Or was it her imagination?

There had been customers to break up the hours. Not a ton but an average amount, she estimated while trying not to admit why the day was moving so slowly.

Gabe.

He hadn't stopped by. Not at all. Not even for a quick pop in.

His absence had left a glaring gap in her usual workday.

She hated that she'd noticed. She hated even more that Liam might be right. Not that she was jealous, per say, but she was envious of the time he was obviously spending with Millie instead of with her.

The urge to lock the door and close the shop early was strong. Although then what?

If Liam was still at the lab working she'd just be sitting alone in her apartment, which seemed even more depressing than being in the shop.

It wasn't like she could call Gabe and ask if he and Millie wanted to come over. Not for the first time and probably not for the last she wished ghosts could have cell phones.

Liam was smart. He studied people's brains. It would be nice if he could use his own brain to figure out some sort of communication system between her and the ghosts. That was most likely impossible but it was nice to dream.

With a sigh she glanced at the clock one more time and snapped to attention when she saw it was just a few minutes before six. For the first time that day she didn't curse the old grandfather clock she'd recently purchased from a local estate sale.

Springing into action Natalie headed for the door and flipped the sign to *Closed*.

Poking her head outside, she checked left and right.

No Gabe or Millie. Though she did see the uniformed ghost of a long ago departed railway employee who walked past the shop to work each morning and home each evening. He always ignored her and since today was no exception, she ignored him as well.

With a sigh she closed and locked the door then turned back to the cash register. It didn't take long to check and record the day's credit card receipts and grab the big bills out of the cash register. She shoved those into a cash bag and stowed that in the safe Liam had bolted to the floor for her under the register.

That was it. Another day gone.

Reaching beneath the counter, she flipped off the stereo, cutting the steady stream of music that pumped through the shop from ten until six every day.

That's when she heard the sound of the television and smiled. Liam was already there, waiting for her. Feeling lighter she moved fast to the door that led to her private apartment in the back.

Swinging the door wide she stopped dead at the sight that greeted her. That being Millie, Gabe and Liam sitting side-by-side on the sofa watching some sort of sports on the television.

"Hey, babe," Liam said, raising his beer to her in a

salute with a quick glance before his eyes went back to the TV.

"Um, hey. What's going on here?"

"Ask him," Liam said, hooking a thumb toward where Gabe sat. By the set of Liam's jaw there was a lot she had missed.

Gabe dropped his hold on Millie's hand and said, "He's still holding a grudge."

Was Gabe being sneaky? He knew Liam couldn't hear him if he wasn't physically touching Millie.

What the hell was going on?

"Um, why?" she asked Gabe.

Liam's head whipped to the side as he said, "I'll tell you why—"

She realized Liam—who hadn't heard Gabe talking about this so-called grudge—thought her question was meant for him.

Liam planted his beer bottle on the coffee table with a clunk. "I was in the lab working."

"Cutting into my body, he means," Gabe elaborated to only her.

"When suddenly Gabe starts screaming, *Ow! Stop! It hurts!*" Liam narrowed his eyes at where she supposed he thought Gabe was sitting, though he missed by a foot or so and instead it looked as if he was just glaring at the stack of books on the side table.

Natalie bit her lip picturing the scene. Liam, scalpel in hand—or perhaps his saw because as horrifying as it was she knew he used a saw a lot in his work—cutting into a cadaver and hearing it scream.

If she didn't know laughing would get her into big trouble with Liam she'd be hysterical by now.

"I'm sorry," she managed between tight lips as she wrestled with the giggles that threatened to surface.

"I see you trying not to laugh," Gabe accused. "You think it's funny too. Come on. Admit it. It was a good joke."

She didn't answer Gabe but she did question Liam. "If you're so angry with him, what are the two of you doing sitting here next to each other on the sofa watching TV together?"

"He's next to me?" Frowning, Liam scooted farther toward the arm of the sofa. "I thought he was sitting in the chair."

"I can't sit next to Millie if I'm in the chair," Gabe explained. "And the view of the TV is better from the sofa."

"Can you please make it so Liam can hear you?" she asked with a frustrated huff. "I thought I was done interpreting for the two of you."

"Sorry." Gabe grabbed Millie's hand.

"And neither one of you has explained how this little gathering came about," she reminded.

"We declared a truce. I promised to never do that to him again," Gabe said. He released Millie's hand and added, "Millie said she won't go back there with me anyway. Seeing my body in pieces freaked her out."

Natalie didn't blame the girl one bit for that.

"And he and Millie agreed to meet with us this evening to chat," Liam added.

"We came over to wait for you to close the shop and I saw he'd turned on the TV. What was I going to do? Not watch the game?" Gabe asked, his hand laced through Millie's again.

"Maybe Millie would prefer to watch something else?" she suggested trying to be a good host.

Gabe waved away her suggestion with his free hand. "She's tired of all those chick movies. She told me Harper leaves them playing all day, on repeat, while she's writing. She's happy to watch anything else. Even college basketball."

Millie's gaze cut to Natalie and she shrugged the delicate shoulders exposed by her flapper dress.

This entire interaction might be the strangest thing Natalie had ever experienced in her life. And she'd met with a prohibition bootlegger inside a secret tunnel and hosted a fake séance with real ghosts for the citizens of Mudville, so that was really saying something.

"All righty. Well, I'm glad you're here." Now maybe she could get some answers.

Chapter Twenty-One

The two men in her life declaring a truce was a big display of growth on both of their parts... Gabe's tendency to let go of Millie's hand so he could comment about Liam to Natalie without the other man hearing notwithstanding. Although she had to admit it was clever, albeit childish.

Drawing in a breath, she moved to the freezer and pulled out two frozen meals. She was starving, but even so, she hesitated. Was it rude to eat in front of their guests?

"Would you mind if we ate?" she asked as she worked to free the two dinners from their boxes before sliding them into the microwave.

"Why would we mind?" Gabe asked.

"Because you can't eat."

"You not eating won't change that," he pointed out.

"All right." Feeling less awkward, she stood and waited for the minutes on the display to count down.

"So what did you and Romeo here want to talk to us about?" Gabe asked.

"I can hear you now. Remember?" Liam scowled.

Gabe winced. "Oh, yeah. I forgot. Sorry."

Liam pouted but said, "It's okay."

"So, Natalie. The reason he invited us?" Gabe reminded.

"I would have invited you myself but you never came into the shop," she pointed out.

"We were busy." Gabe shrugged.

Hiding her hurt, she said, "Oh. Yeah. That's what I figured..."

Liam shot her a sideways glance but remained silent.

"I just thought we could talk about stuff." She shrugged again.

"Ghost stuff?" Gabe asked.

"Sure. And other stuff too. Whatever."

At the ding, she was grateful for the interruption. She knew Millie didn't like talking about her death and that's exactly what Natalie was going to ask her about.

Taking advantage of the reprieve, she slid one

microwaveable dish onto the cocktail table in front of Liam with a fork and a paper towel in lieu of the paper napkins she'd run out of.

She placed her own down on the side table before sitting in the empty chair.

"Gourmet meal, I see," Gabe snarked.

Emerald eyes beneath one dark raised brow cut to Natalie. "He always like this?"

"Yup." Natalie nodded.

"I guess I wasn't missing that much when I couldn't hear him," Liam said while lifting one steaming bite of Salisbury steak on his fork.

"I told you that you weren't."

"Um, still here. Thanks. And still can hear you," Gabe said.

Meanwhile Millie just watched the action, like she was in the stands observing some Victorian lawn tennis match. She was definitely a quiet one as she sat next to Gabe, her posture upright and her ankles crossed.

Prim. Proper. Quiet. Pretty much the opposite of Natalie. Is that what Gabe liked about her?

Natalie cleared her throat and decided to get the conversation back on track before it devolved any further. "So, Gabe, Millie, it was me mostly who wanted to talk."

"And I'm still not sure about what," Gabe said.

Natalie turned her gaze on Millie. "You."

Her lipstick reddened mouth formed a surprised *oh* before she asked, "Me?"

"Yes. You've fascinated me since the first time I set eyes on you."

"Why?" Millie drew back like this was an unwelcome discovery. As if this—or any—attention focused on her was unwelcome.

"She's a little shy," Gabe explained.

A little? Ha! That was the understatement of the century—

That thought knocked some sense into Natalie. Millie wasn't from this century.

She'd been born and raised at the turn of the last century when all youth spoke when spoken to. And women went from their father's house and control to their husband's where they remained subservient— financially, socially, politically—for the rest of their lives.

Except, judging by her youthful appearance, Millie hadn't lived long enough for all that.

And if the style of her short flapper dress and bobbed hair was any indication, she'd died right when things for women had just begun to change, even if slightly and slowly, when they finally were allowed to vote.

As Natalie tried to craft a question that wouldn't send the girl fluttering away like a frightened bird—because she really did look ready to bolt—Gabe turned to face Millie.

"I think she probably wants to know how you died," Gabe began as the girl's eyes widened. Holding both of Millie's hands in his now, Gabe looked up at Natalie. "But that's because I haven't had a chance to tell her yet that you don't remember."

"Oh. I understand." Natalie nodded hiding her disappointment even though she should have expected it. Gabe didn't remember the exact moment of his death either.

"Here's a question you might be able to answer. Why are you in a party dress?" Natalie asked.

"Oh. This." The slightest smile curved her mouth. "It was New Year's Eve nineteen-nineteen. That new law banning alcohol—"

"Prohibition," Liam said softly.

"Yes." Millie nodded. "That was to start January first so the owners of the house threw the biggest party. My friend invited me. I didn't even know anyone there. I had to lie to my parents and tell them we were staying in Sharon Springs. They never would have let me travel all the way to Mudville. The party was amazing. There was so much food and drinks and music and dancing. They hired a whole jazz band from Binghamton," she added with awe.

"And that's why someone carved the date nineteen-twenty into the woodwork in the bedroom?" Natalie guessed.

Millie shook her head. "I don't know anything about that. I would never. And if I saw any of the college boys doing it I would have told them not to."

"College boys?" Gabe looked slightly horrified as he asked, "Were you in college?"

"Oh, no. My family wasn't wealthy enough to send me."

"So exactly how young are you?" Gabe asked.

"Twenty."

"Jeezus." Gabe let go of her to run his hands over his face.

"You dog, you." Liam grinned.

Natalie sent Liam a glare. "Stop. She might look twenty but she's actually like a hundred."

"One hundred and twenty-four," Liam corrected. "If she died that night."

"Whatever." Natalie frowned at Liam for using math against her. He knew she hated numbers.

Ignoring the two men—Gabe, who still looked a bit shell-shocked he was dating a girl young enough to be his daughter, and Liam, who was being his usual smart-ass self—Natalie turned back to Millie.

"You're still in your party dress—and you look absolutely lovely, by the way. Just beautiful—but that makes me think, did you die that night? At the party?" she asked, keeping her voice gentle.

Millie's eyes dropped away before she brought them back up.

"I don't remember anything past midnight."

Chapter Twenty-Two

"We spent like an hour at the last LADS meeting discussing what that nineteen-twenty scratched in the woodwork could mean and how it got there. And now that I'm pretty sure it happened at that huge pre-Prohibition New Year's party, I can't even tell Harper."

The frustration of it was robbing Natalie of all enjoyment of her post-dinner tea and book now that Gabe and Millie had gone.

Liam glanced up from the television, a bottle of beer, his after-dinner beverage of choice, in his hand. "Why is that? Why can't you tell Harper?"

"Um, hello. Ghosts."

What was she supposed to say to explain how she knew that information? Without proof. Short of finding a diary or news article or some written documentation how could she possibly know if not from her ability to ask someone who'd been there? Died there...

With a distinct look of annoyance, Liam said, "That's what I mean. Why haven't you ever told Harper you can talk to ghosts? You're friends."

"Um, because she would have thought I was losing my mind."

"You told me," he reminded.

"Yeah, well, at the time I didn't care if you thought I was delusional. And I was trying to make up for reporting you to the sheriff."

He bobbed his head to the side. "I'll concede that point, but don't you see? Things are different now. There's proof. She'll be able to actually hear Gabe and Millie. She'll know it's true."

"She'll also know I've been lying to her since last summer." Natalie could barely count all the times she'd lied to Harper. One of her best—one of her very few—living friends here.

"You can just explain—" Liam began.

"No," she interrupted.

"Fine. Suit yourself." He raised the bottle to his lips as his gaze moved back to the television.

If she weren't so engrossed in the newest

bestselling book the reading world was all agog over she might have been more annoyed with Liam for watching sports on her television even after his new game-watching buddy Gabe had left.

Gabe and Millie were heading back to the house where they'd all sheltered during the exorcism scare.

Now that they could be heard when they touched—and they were almost always touching—it was better they didn't hang out at Agnes's house where they might spook Harper again. Natalie didn't have the energy for another cleansing session with Madame Letisha.

Apparently the house on the hill was not only huge, but the older couple who owned it had plenty of rooms that they rarely if ever used. And they had a dog.

According to Gabe, Millie liked dogs. Much more than she liked Agnes's pet pig Petunia, which scared her and was, she was told, sometimes allowed inside the house.

After hearing Harper and Alice Mudd both talk about the dead body the pigs on the farm had so efficiently disposed of years ago, Natalie was going to look at pigs a little differently herself.

With her internal ruminations about pigs concluded, Natalie reopened her book and was about to lose herself once again in the story of one young woman's life-and-death battles in a land of dragons and magic when Liam's cell phone pinged.

Frowning she glanced up. Who could be texting her boyfriend at this hour?

He stood so he could extricate the cell from the pocket of his pants. She watched as he sat again and read the screen, before typing in a reply. Then he tossed the cell—face down—on the coffee table in front of him and picked up his beer again.

No explanation. No answer to who it was. Of course, she hadn't asked, but still...

The book and its complex plot, immense cast of characters and sweeping world-building held no interest for her any longer. Not when real life intrigue was playing out before her.

Finally, when she could no longer stand it, she asked, "Who was that texting so late?"

"It's not late." He shot her a frown. "It's not even eight."

That was not an answer. Her heart began to pound as her imagination went wild.

"All right, it's not that late. But who was it?" she asked again.

He glanced at her and said, "Stone. Why?"

"No reason. Just curious."

Stone? They weren't friends. They'd never texted each other in all the months since they'd met. At least as far as she knew.

"Since when do you and Stone text each other?" she asked, laying the book down and completely abandoning any hope of being able to concentrate on the story after this. "How does he even have your number?"

"We exchanged numbers when we were at the house for that... ghost thing," he said, the frown creasing his brow.

"So why is he texting you now?" she asked, unable to let this rest.

Liam let out a sigh. He reached for the remote and muted the television, finally, then turned to her. "I'm meeting him at the Muddy River Inn tomorrow."

"Oh. That sounds fun. Maybe I'll join you."

He shook his head. "We're meeting early. At four-thirty. The shop will still be open. And with Jules out sick, you'll have to work."

"I'll come over at six after I close. You should still be there, right? Or I could close early if it's slow."

"I doubt we'll hang out past six. He'll want to get home to Harper for dinner."

"Harper can meet us. We can all have dinner there together."

Liam grimaced. "Nat. We just want to have a couple of beers. Just us guys. Okay?"

Secret texts. Meet-ups she wasn't invited to. That's it. She was certain. Liam was cheating on her.

"Oh... Okay," she said, tasting bile in the back of her throat.

She was going to vomit Salisbury steak, mashed potatoes, green beans and apple cobbler all over the floor if the panicked churning of her stomach was any indication.

Liam laughed. "Natalie. You don't have to look like that. I just asked if I could have one guy's night out with Stone. Am I not allowed to?"

"You're allowed." Her voice sounded way too high. She consciously lowered it as she said, "I'll be happy if you and Stone become friends. Why wouldn't I be?"

If it was Stone he was meeting...

She had to know for sure. She couldn't survive with the doubt if she didn't know.

And she knew one surefire way to find out.

Chapter Twenty-Three

The following morning was torture for Natalie.

She opened the store at ten, but no Gabe. She unpacked a delivery of wine and rearranged the front table's books, but still no Gabe.

Lunchtime passed, but she felt too sick to her stomach to even eat one of the granola bars she kept stashed under the counter. Her morning coffee hadn't set too well in her belly either.

Customers came and went. The cat disappeared and reappeared again, all while generally ignoring her as usual. The crow made an appearance to harass her from the roof for a bit but still no Gabe.

As the afternoon wore on she began to panic. No Gabe meant no one to spy on Liam for her.

She'd have to close the shop and drive over to the bar. Then peer through the window to see who Liam was actually meeting there. If he was there at all and not meeting his lover in some *pied-à-terre*—some love nest—somewhere nearby.

But the windows of the bar were high. She'd never be able to see in through them.

She'd have to put on some sort of a disguise so he wouldn't recognize her—at least a hat and sunglasses—and peek in through the doorway.

"Hey, Nat."

She spun to see Gabe had sauntered through the door and was currently taking a moment to peruse the new front display, as if her whole world wasn't currently ending.

"Oh my God. What took you so long? I thought you'd never get here."

"What's wrong? What happened?" He moved immediately closer, looking concerned.

"Liam is cheating on me."

"What? What happened? How do you know?"

"He got a text last night."

"And?"

"And when I asked him about it he acted all... cagey. Finally he said it was Stone."

"Okay..." Gabe said slowly.

"He said they're meeting for a beer. *Just the guys,*" she said in an unflattering imitation of Liam's voice.

Gabe hesitated, waiting. Finally, he said, "That's it?"

"What do you mean, *that's it*? I asked if I could come too and he basically said no."

"And that means he's cheating on you?"

"He could be. That's why I need you to find out for sure."

"Why me? Can't you just ask Harper if Stone is meeting Liam?"

She drew back in horror. "And admit to a woman in a perfect relationship that I'm such a loser that my boyfriend is cheating on me? Besides, men lie for each other. Liam might have told Stone to tell Harper they were together."

Gabe scowled. "None of that logic makes any sense. But if you don't want to ask Harper then just call the bar and ask if Liam and Stone are there."

"Maybe he bribed the bartender to say he's there even if he's not," she suggested.

"How would that even work? You could ask to speak with him or show up there."

"If I did that, then the bartender could just say, *sorry, he just left.*"

"You have an incredibly active imagination." Gabe

huffed out a breath. "You could be completely wrong about this and Liam is actually just going to hang out with Stone."

"And you are in the perfect position to prove to me that I'm wrong, so why don't you do it? Go over and see if they're at the bar. You like being right. I'll even let you say *I told you so* as often as you want if I am wrong. I promise."

Gabe shook his head. "I really don't feel comfortable—"

"Gabe! Please."

"Natalie, think about it. What if he is? Cheating. And I'm not saying he is because I don't think he is but if by some wild stretch of the imagination he is, then *I* have to be the one to tell you and break your heart. Is that fair to me?"

"Fair to you? This has nothing to do with you." Didn't he see that she was a mess?

"It has everything to do with me," Gabe countered. "Think about it. If you somehow found out Stone was cheating on Harper, would *you* want to be the one to tell her?"

"I wouldn't *want* to, but I'd know I should so I would do it. I'd have to. It would be hard but it's the right thing to do. She has a right to know." Natalie's eyes flew wide. "Wait. *Is* Stone cheating on Harper? Did you see something? Did Millie tell you?"

"Jeezus. What goes on in your mind, woman? Do you always jump to the worst possible scenario?"

Gabe pressed both hands to his head as if this conversation was giving him a headache.

Welcome to the club, buddy. Her head had hurt since last night after that text came in.

"And no. Stone's not cheating. He's a farmer. Do you know how hard they work? I don't think he'd have the energy to have an affair *and* handle Harper, who's a handful, I can tell you. I know. I spent some time in that house." Gabe shook his head. "You need to relax."

Natalie folded her arms across her chest. "I will relax. *After* you go to the bar and see for yourself that Stone and Liam are there and this is all as innocent as you say it is. *And* if you tell me what they're talking about."

Gabe's eyes flashed. "No. That's pushing it too far."

She scowled. "Fine. So then I guess asking you to look around the warehouse for any evidence is out of the question?"

Breathing in through his nose with his lips pressed into an unhappy line, Gabe narrowed his eyes at her in a glare that gave her his answer to that question.

"I'll go and see if they're at the bar just to appease you. I will *not* spy on what they're talking about. And I will *not* go poking through his things at the warehouse. There's a bro code, you know."

A bro code which apparently spanned into the afterlife, even for guys who until recently had never spoken and couldn't stand each other... but she would take what she could get.

"Okay, deal," she said.

"Deal," Gabe echoed with less enthusiasm.

Natalie glanced at the clock and then back to Gabe. "You'd better get going. He said they're meeting at four-thirty."

"Fine." Gabe let out a breath and pinned Natalie with a glare. "*You* are a lot of work."

"Right back at you, bro," Natalie said, heavy on the attitude.

Now all she had to do was manage to not hyperventilate until Gabe returned with his report.

Chapter Twenty-Four

WAITING WAS NOT HER STRONG SUIT. Waiting on an afternoon when the shop was abnormally slow and she was just an hour from closing had proved impossible.

With the door locked, the lights out and the *Closed* sign visible, Natalie pretended it wasn't five rather than six and crept outside through the back door.

Like a thief, she waited for the car coming down the side street to pass then took off at a run across the train tracks to the door of the warehouse-turned-cadaver-lab.

It was ridiculous that Gabe wouldn't search the lab for her. She knew he'd gone poking in Liam's stuff before. But after his reluctance today she had to be grateful he even agreed to go to the bar.

Not only because Gabe was being less than cooperative but also because he wouldn't have been able to snoop as thoroughly as she could anyway, she'd decided to take on the job of searching Liam's lab and living space herself.

She could get in. No problem. She'd seen Liam punch in the code on the door lock at least a dozen times.

Natalie enjoyed the romance of having the old original skeleton keys to the train depot, but she had to admit this modern keypad was super convenient for breaking and entering to spy on one's boyfriend.

Once inside she punched in the code to turn off the alarm system which she'd seen Liam do, as well. Not to mention it was the same code as the front door lock. That was his bad for not being more creative.

She avoided the table with Gabe's body on it, even though it was covered in plastic. It was just too creepy seeing him cut open on a table after having watched him walk around Mudville whole, dressed and seemingly alive—in ghost form at least—for so many months.

Keeping her eyes focused on anything but Gabe's earthly remains, she focused on the two doors that led to the non-cadaver filled areas of the building.

One room was used as an office. The other, as

Liam's bedroom-slash-living space. She went there first. If he were hiding anything from her—such as another woman's panties or love notes—that was the most likely place.

The door was closed but the knob turned easily in her hand.

Inside the room, where she'd been before but not often because—*ick*, cadaver lab—she glanced around.

The man was nearly inhuman. Who made their bed so neatly? Like seriously, she could probably bounce a quarter on the bedding it was tucked in so tightly.

There wasn't a closet but that didn't seem to matter. His clothes were folded on the open shelving as neatly as a Gap store with too many employees on a slow night.

Below, lined up on the floor in perfect formation were a pair of running shoes next to the rubber-soled clog-like monstrosities he had said were from his med school days when she'd questioned him about them.

There was one side table next to the bed that had three drawers. Excited this could yield something, she tried the top drawer and found hand cream, tissues, pain killers, nail clippers, assorted pens, a pad of paper, and the Valentine's Day card she had given him.

Nothing exciting and actually, pretty sparce offerings as far as junk drawers went.

The next two drawers were even more disappointing. One contained underwear, rolled up tightly like multicolored cotton sausages and stored in rows. In the other drawer pairs of socks had been given the same treatment as the underwear above them.

She shook her head, wondering which one of them was normal. Her with overstuffed messy drawers she could barely close, or him with his psychopathic level of organization.

That led to her next thought and it was a horrifying one. How in the world could two people who were so different hope to survive for the long term? Either her messiness would get to him or his neatness would get to her. Then, when it was too much to bear, then what?

She didn't have much time to fully go down that rabbit hole because she heard the knob jiggle on the front door.

Oh, no!

Was Liam back already? And so fast? It wasn't even five-thirty. He'd barely been gone an hour.

Turning back to slide the drawer closed as quietly as possible, she weighed her options.

The window in the room was old. Opening it

would cause a racket, if she could even get it open and it hadn't been painted shut long ago.

There was no other way out but the door, which was in clear sight of the entrance.

She was trapped. Unless she was super lucky and he went directly into the office. Then maybe she could slip out of the bedroom and then outside. He might hear the front door but she could duck behind the building and hide. Then make a run for the shop and pretend she'd never been there.

It was a good plan until the room's door flung wide and the man standing there looked as surprised to see her as she was to see him and that was because he was *not* Liam.

WHEN THE HELL HAD LIAM INSTALLED A freezer in the lab?

Natalie didn't remember it being there before, but she was sure aware of it now that she was inside it.

Lucky her. Liam had chosen a nice big one so the intruder had no problem flinging aside the empty shelves, shoving her in, and then slamming the door.

The door she couldn't open.

She'd been trying since she'd heard the door to the outside slam—how long ago? She didn't know.

Time was beginning to have no meaning in the cold dark interior of the freezer.

It was so dark. So cold. What her body was doing could barely be called shivering anymore. She'd surpassed *shiver* a while ago. The extreme level of vibration of her body now deserved a whole other level of description.

Trying not to cry and waste what little oxygen might remain in there with her she resorted to repeating silently in her mind over and over again *I will not die, I will not die, I will not die.*

The refrain cut off when her brain went rogue and threw in a different variation.

I'm going to die.

There. Inside this freezer. All because she didn't trust Liam.

Death by foolishness—

"Natalie? You here?"

The sound was muffled by the appliance—of course, Liam had bought the best freezer he could with thick walls and a nice tight seal—but she heard well enough to know that voice anywhere.

It was Gabe. He was here. She was saved.

"Gabe!" She kicked with her foot and pounded with the fist pinned against her in the tight space.

"Where are you?" he asked.

"Inside the freezer."

"What the hell? Why?" His voice was louder now. He had to be right against the door.

"There was a burglar. He put me in here. I can't get out. I tried."

"Shit. There's a built-in hasp in the handle to put a padlock. It looks like he jammed like a four-inch carpentry nail in there and then bent it. It's keeping the door from opening," Gabe told her.

That was it then. She was back to knowing she was going to die.

Gabe wouldn't be able to open the freezer door. He couldn't unbend a big bent nail, even with his new ghost power.

Resigned to her fate, she decided to make the best of it and said, "Gabe?"

"Yeah?"

"Quick, tell me before I die. Was Liam really at the bar with Stone?"

"Oh my God. Yes, you ridiculous woman. He was there with Stone. He's not cheating on you. Now, hang tight. I'll be right back with help. I promise. And once you're free I'm going to insist that you seriously reevaluate your priorities."

The silence that followed Gabe's departure surrounded her like a shroud. She should have told him to stay. At least she would have had company until the end...

Time passed, though she had no idea how long. It was enough that she began to doubt she was truly going to be rescued at all in spite of Gabe's promise.

The part of her brain still functioning went back to wondering how long she'd been in there. Then turned to wishing she knew as much about the human body as Liam did. If she did then she might be able to estimate how much longer she could survive in there.

Long enough for Gabe to return with help? She didn't know.

She turned to a subject she did know at least a little bit though not enough about—ghosts.

Would she become a ghost too, destined to spend the rest of eternity haunting the warehouse?

That might not be so bad. She could hang out with Gabe and the others. But it would suck watching Liam date other women.

Would Liam be able to hear her ghost because they'd been in love? Or would Gabe and Millie—in an ironic twist of fate—have to act as the go-between for her and Liam?

Sleep called to her. She closed her eyes since it was too dark to see anyway and absently noted that she'd stopped shivering.

That was good. It would be easier to sleep...

The sound of a door slamming against the wall startled her mostly awake.

"Natalie! I'm coming, baby!" Hearing the voice of the man she loved had her straining to focus.

"Liam?" She couldn't yell—she didn't seem to have the air in her lungs to—but that was okay. He was here. She was rescued.

"What the hell? Okay. Don't talk, baby. I'll have you out in a second... Shit! There's something jamming the door handle. Just hang on, baby!"

It was quiet again. The disappointment would have brought tears to her eyes but she didn't seem to have any tears left. Maybe they were frozen.

Her thoughts, fuzzy though they were, were interrupted by the overwhelming amount of loud banging and cursing going on outside the box that had become her world for the past—however long.

One extra loud clang vibrated her and everything around her before the door swung wide letting warm air and blinding light flood inside.

Squinting against the painful glare, her eyes finally adjusted enough she could see. And there stood Liam wielding a sledgehammer like an avenging angel. Parts of the freezer's mangled handle littered the floor at his feet.

Gabe, looking equal parts concerned and relieved, stood next to him.

It was the most wonderful sight she'd ever seen.

She tried to move and found not only that it hurt, but that her limbs refused to cooperate.

It took Liam's strength to get her out of the freezer as Gabe stood by helpless. Only with Liam's help did she make it to the chair in his office.

Squatting down to be eye level with her, he rubbed her arms and then her hands with his own to warm her.

His gaze never wavering as he studied her, Liam asked, "Are you all right?"

She realized his single-minded focus was less love inspired and more the doctor in him coming out as he checked her pupils then laid a thumb against the pulse at her wrist.

Doctor William Walsh and all his medical training, useful though it was, wasn't what she needed right now. She needed her boyfriend Liam and his warm strong arms to protect her and make her believe everything was all right.

"W-w-when did you get a freezer?" she asked, teeth chattering as her whole body began to vibrate once again.

"I'm going to start getting some fresh brains—" Liam began.

She drew back, cringing. Even half frozen she couldn't deal with talking about that.

Liam shook his head. "Never mind. You don't need the details."

"Definitely d-don't," she managed as he pulled her close again.

She sank gratefully against him.

"Oh my God. You are absolutely freezing," he said, rubbing her more.

She didn't disagree as she tried to absorb the warmth from Liam's body pressed against her and the friction of his hands.

"I thought I was going to lose my mind when Gabe and Millie came in and told me. I'm lucky I didn't get pulled over for driving eighty down Main Street. I don't even know what Stone thinks of me for running out on him like that. It's not like I could explain your ghost friend was whispering in my ear that you were trapped in the freezer. If Gabe hadn't found you. Or hadn't been able to tell me..." Liam let the sentence trail off.

"I would have suffocated," Natalie finished for him.

"Extreme cold slows respiration and heartrate so you probably would have frozen to death before—" When her eyes popped wide Liam cringed. "Um, never mind. But Natalie, how the hell did this happen? How did you get stuck inside the freezer? What were you even doing here?"

Skipping over the part when she'd broken in

herself, Natalie began with, "A man broke into your lab. He shoved me in there."

Liam shook his head. "So this was a *robbery*?"

"I don't know. All I know is I thought I was going to *die*—" Her voice broke on a sob, not only because of how close she'd come to death, but also because Liam couldn't be mad at a crying woman. Right?

"It's okay. You're okay. You're safe now. I'm here." Even as he comforted her with one arm, Liam reached for the computer keyboard on the desk with his other.

"What are you doing?" she asked when she realized she was no longer the center of his attention.

"I'm checking the security cameras."

Uh, oh.

He was going to see her sneaking in.

She cut her gaze to Gabe whose brows rose.

He knew she'd broken in. She'd asked him to search the lab and he'd said no. He was a smart guy. He had to know exactly what she was doing inside the lab while Liam wasn't there. It was probably why he'd come looking for her there in the first place when he didn't find her in the shop.

Meanwhile, a view of the front door camera feed came up on Liam's computer screen.

How could she forget he'd said he was going to get security cameras? That promise—or threat—had come after he caught the old ladies in town peeking in his windows. Back when everyone thought he was a serial killer because of all the bodies being carried into the lab.

In her defense, that had been almost a year ago and she'd never actually seen any cameras. They must be hidden well.

She was about to be caught.

Why would he bother with a security system? What was there to steal? Body parts? Although to be fair, someone had broken in.

Two people, actually. Just today if she counted herself.

She knew why she'd done it, but what had the guy who'd almost cost her life wanted?

"Mother fucker," Liam bit out.

Oh, boy. He must have seen her during his scrolling of the feed and did he sound mad. She could only hope he would take into consideration that she almost died and forgive her snooping.

Liam leaned back and drew in an angry, nostril-flaring breath. Tipping his head toward the frozen image of a man on the screen, he said, "I know him. He's the one applying for the same grant I am. The deadline for submission is coming up. I've been working like a dog trying to get it done—"

She nodded. "Which is why you were so cranky."

Liam frowned. "I wouldn't exactly say cranky…"

"Tomato, tomahto," she said dismissively, feeling so much better.

Liam hadn't been cheating. And he didn't seem mad at her at all. He was angry at the guy on the screen.

"But why would he break in here? And then lock me in the freezer?" she asked.

"I bet that bastard came to steal my proposal. My Jeep was gone. He probably thought the lab was empty. He must have panicked when he found you in here. He couldn't get caught—it would be a career-ender—and you could identify him. So…the freezer."

Natalie shook her head. "That's unbelievable."

Gabe let out a snort. "It's fucked up."

"People will do a lot for half a million dollars," Liam explained.

"I wouldn't." She frowned.

Half a million? That's all? This guy was willing to kill someone for five hundred grand. That wouldn't even buy a shoe-box sized apartment in Manhattan.

It was actually kind of insulting that her life wasn't even worth a cool million!

Gabe raised one hand. "Um, I just remembered something I probably should have mentioned earlier."

Natalie turned to him expectantly.

"That day I came to say goodbye to Ethel and Myra before Doctor Death shipped them out, they mentioned that some guy had been snooping around the building. He tried the door but it was locked. And he was looking in the windows. Trying to open them. Then he left."

But this time when he tried, the door was unlocked and the alarm disabled because of her. She'd almost been the orchestrator of her own demise.

"Oh, shit," she breathed when that realization hit.

Liam frowned. "What? What's happening?"

"Gabe was just telling me—" Natalie began.

"Hold up a minute. Why can't I hear him anymore?" Liam asked.

"Millie's not here," Natalie explained.

Gabe elaborated, "She said seeing my dismembered body again, left out on the table under plastic like I'm some piece of leftover meatloaf, is too much for her to deal with."

Natalie rolled her eyes. "She didn't say that."

"She would have if they'd had plastic wrap and meatloaf while she'd been alive."

"Um, hello. Still can't hear what he's saying." Liam scowled.

She turned back to Liam who was visibly annoyed.

"Sorry. Anyway, the two old lady cadaver ghosts told him there was some guy trying to get in last week."

Slow seething anger colored his features and his cheeks. "The night the alarm went off. You were out and I was waiting for you at your place."

Natalie nodded. She remembered.

It was the first LADS meeting. At Harper and Agnes's house. The night she first saw Millie— She didn't have time to think more about it because Liam was on the move.

Grumbling another string of curses worthy of a sailor even though he'd been in the Army, Liam stood. The angry determined set of his jaw made her happy his wrath was directed at this other researcher and not at her.

Kneeling, Liam flipped up the embroidered Army-logo cloth draped over what she'd always thought was just a side table. She saw now it was a safe.

As Liam keyed in the code, he glanced up. "Can Gabe make sure you get back to your place okay?"

"Why?" When she saw him pull out a gun, she swallowed. "Liam. What are you going to do?"

"Kill him," he said with an eerie level of calm as he checked the gun for bullets.

He strapped on the shoulder holster, complete with gun and extra clip of ammunition.

When he grabbed his jacket off a wall hook and pulled it on over the holster, Natalie began to panic in earnest.

"You're not really. Are you?"

With the hardest look she'd ever seen in his eyes he said, "I'll see how I feel when I find him."

Zipping the jacket, he glanced back at her from the office doorway. "And when I get back, we're going to discuss why you were sneaking into the lab while I was at the bar."

When he was gone, the exterior door slamming shut hard behind him, Gabe let out a low whistle. "Damn."

Still in shock over Liam snapping into warrior mode, she said, "You can say that again."

"He kind of makes me glad I'm already dead," Gabe continued.

She could only hope that thief of a researcher wouldn't be joining Gabe in the realm of the dead.

The intruder deserved prosecution. No doubt. Public shaming by all those in his field. Definitely. But even after what he'd done to her, she couldn't believe he deserved death. Especially if it would send Liam to prison.

Gabe took a step toward the doorway and Natalie followed.

As they made their way past the freezer, Natalie shoved the door closed with more force than necessary. When the door refused to stay shut because of its lack of handle, she reached behind the appliance and yanked the plug out of the wall socket.

Once she'd taken out her frustration and worry on the freezer she turned back to Gabe as he asked, "You don't think he'd do it, do you?"

Feeling a little sick, and not from her time in the freezer, she said, "I wish I knew."

Chapter Twenty-Six

Waiting was hell.

It didn't matter that Natalie wasn't inside a freezer praying to be rescued, but rather in her nice warm apartment pacing, waiting for Liam to return. She felt like she was losing her mind as she repeatedly checked her cell for at least a text if not a call.

Gabe and Millie sat in front of the television but they were watching her back and forth progress across the room instead of the home improvement show on TV.

"If you don't stop pacing, you're going to wear a hole in that rug."

As if Gabe had cursed her, Natalie tripped on a wrinkle in the throw rug and had to catch herself to stop from falling. She sent him a glare.

He shrugged. "Told you."

"Why hasn't he called?" she asked, moving from plain old debilitating worry to full on panic.

It had been hours. Hours during which any number of things could have happened. And none of the scenarios that Natalie could come up with were good.

Midnight had come and gone. The sun hadn't risen yet but technically it was tomorrow, which to her mind made it feel like Liam had been missing for like two days instead of just since last evening.

The glow of headlights hitting the closed curtains had her rushing to the window.

"He's home," she breathed when she saw Liam's Jeep pull in and park by the warehouse.

"See. I told you," Gabe said, but even after his condescending *I told you so*, he looked relieved himself.

She was about to run outside in her fuzzy slippers when Liam turned and started walking toward her and the back door of the depot instead of toward the lab.

His progress across the short distance felt like it took forever but he finally made it to her. Close enough she could yell at him for disappearing as worry and relief began to make way for other emotions.

"I was so worried. Why didn't you call or text?" she asked as he pushed past her and into the room.

"I was too pissed off to talk."

"At the researcher guy?" she asked, hoping it wasn't her he was so angry with he didn't even want to speak to her.

"Who else would it be?" He tossed his jacket on the back of a chair then reached into the fridge for a bottle of beer.

Twisting off the cap, he tossed it into the trash and took a long swallow right where he stood illuminated by the refrigerator's glow. Only then did he close the fridge door and head for the sofa.

His determined stride and ramrod posture showed he was still strung tight.

Flopping backward onto the cushions, Liam almost sat in Gabe's lap. Only some quick reflexes on the ghost's part got him clear in time.

Gabe relocated to the empty spot on the other side of Millie but remained quiet.

Natalie couldn't blame him. She wasn't sure if she wanted to disturb Liam in this mood either but she had to. The curiosity was killing her.

"So, um, what happened?" she dared to ask.

His gaze cut to hers. "I didn't kill him if that's what you're asking."

There was a collective sigh audible from the three of them in the room. Natalie, Gabe and even Millie.

Liam's only reaction to the sound that alerted him that they weren't alone was a barely perceptible pause as he lifted the bottle to his mouth.

"Were you even able to find him?" Natalie asked.

"Oh, I found him all right." Jaw set, Liam raised the rapidly emptying bottle to his lips one more time.

Gabe moved so he was no longer touching Millie—the move his own personal mute button when it came to Liam—and said, "Getting a story out of this guy is like pulling teeth."

Natalie did her best to not react to the truth of that and focused her attention on Liam. "And did you confront him?"

"It was hard to since the police were hauling him away in handcuffs at the time."

"You went to the police?" she asked, surprised and relieved at the same time.

He sighed. "Yeah. It took everything I had to not beat the shit out of him first, but I brought the video of him entering my lab to the police instead. And, sorry about this, Nat, but you'll be getting a call from the Albany police to give a statement. I told them how he assaulted you and endangered your life."

"Don't apologize. It's fine. Of course I'll give a statement." She moved to where he sat and perched on the arm since the rest of the sofa was occupied. Laying a hand on his arm, she said, "I'm proud of you."

His brows formed a low line above his eyes as he grunted.

"Looking back later, you'll be happy you took the high road," she continued.

He let out a snort. "Not exactly the high road."

"Why? What else did you do?" she accused.

"I might have sent the video of him breaking and entering along with a copy of the police report to the grant committee... And my med school alumni association mailing list. And then I might have stolen the envelope containing his grant application off his desk."

"Liam!" Natalie drew in a gasp as Gabe let out a loud bark of a laugh that resonated audibly through the room since his hand was on Millie's leg.

Liam cocked up a brow. "See. My man Gabe approves."

"I didn't say I didn't approve," Natalie said. "There should be ramifications after what he did. I just don't want any of this to blow back on you."

"It won't. I promise."

"What about your research? He wasn't able to take anything of yours, was he?" She didn't know. She was locked inside a freezer at the time.

"Thank God I took the precaution of locking up my application in the safe."

Her eyes widened. "But what about your computer? Can he get in there?"

Liam shook his head. "I have all my research backed up on a hard drive but I keep that in the safe. The computer itself requires a thumbprint plus all of the files are password protected. A little paranoia goes a long way. But thank you for worrying about me."

Grabbing one arm he tugged her lower so he could kiss her lips before releasing her and saying, "So now that that worry has been taken care of, let's talk about *you* being in my lab."

"Uh, oh. Time for us to go. See you later, Nat." Gabe stood and pulled Millie up after him. Then they both swooped toward the wall.

"Traitor," she mumbled. Was it too much to ask for some back up from her supposed friend?

Liam pulled her down into his lap. "Talk."

Avoiding looking directly into his eyes that seemed to see too much, she asked, "Are you mad at me?"

"That you almost got yourself killed? Yes, very. That you were in the warehouse, no. Not at all. But I am curious. So?" He paused and waited.

There was no avoiding it. She let out a sigh and

rushed to explain, "You were so elusive about that text and wouldn't let me meet Stone with you that..."

"That what?" he asked before his eyes widened. "You thought I was cheating on you?"

She avoided eye contact as she admitted, "Maybe the thought might have crossed my mind."

"Natalie!"

"I'm sorry. You were just being so secretive."

"There was good reason for that." He sighed and wrestled his cell out of his back pocket, jostling her in the process but not enough for her to move.

She might never sit in his lap again if he was mad at her for not trusting him, for doubting them, so she held tight.

When the cell was finally out, he scrolled through a few pictures then turned the phone to face her.

"What is that?" she asked.

"The design for your new garden."

"My what?" She took the cell and looked closer.

"Stone's father does garden design. That's what I was meeting with him about and why I couldn't let you come. Stone's going to plant it for you. I was going to surprise you."

"You were?" Her voice cracked with emotion.

"I was. But as it turns out you're impossible to

surprise." His raised brows had a distinctly judgmental look to them.

"I'm sorry," she said, her heart aching. He'd done an incredibly sweet thing and she'd ruined it.

"It's fine. But jeezus, Natalie. For future reference I'm never gonna cheat on you. I know what that feels like and I wouldn't do that to you or anybody."

"I know." She nodded. His wife's cheating was the reason for his divorce. He'd told her that.

"No." He shook his head. "You obviously don't. I have the video evidence. Proof that you don't know I would never cheat on you."

She hung her head in shame.

"Hey," he said, lifting her chin. "I love you."

"Are you sure?" she asked.

It was an honest question. Leave it to her to ruin a good thing with her insecurity.

"Yeah. I'm sure. I tried not to but it seems it's impossible for me not to love you."

She smiled sadly. "I guess I'm glad about that."

He cupped her face, brushing a thumb over her jaw. "How are you feeling after your time in the freezer?"

"All right." Now that he was home and had forgiven her and she knew he wasn't cheating, everything was perfect. She hardly even remembered her time in the deep freeze.

"You sure? No frost bite? All extremities are intact?"

She didn't admit that she hadn't actually checked for signs of frostbite, not that she'd know what to look for anyway. Instead she said, "Yes. All good."

"Good." He nodded. "Now, get up. Let's get you to bed."

"I'm okay. I'm not tired." Opening the shop tomorrow morning was going to be hell but she was too keyed up to go to sleep yet.

"I didn't say anything about sleep." He stood and grabbed her hand. "I feel the need to convince you how much I love you. And convince myself you're actually all right after I nearly lost you today. You okay with that?"

It seemed like secretive Liam was gone, as was stressed out Liam. Amorous though bossy Liam was back and all was right with the world.

She nodded as a small smile tipped up her lips. "Yeah. I'm okay with that."

"So we're invited to a party," Natalie told Liam over dinner.

"Oh? Where? Harper's?" he guessed.

"Not exactly." She cringed.

Liam frowned. "What's up? Why are you looking at me like that?"

"How would you feel about attending a ghost party?" she asked.

His brows shot up. "A ghost party," he repeated.

"Yeah. They used to have them in the cemetery across from the variety store on Main Street. But this one is at the big house on the hill where all the ghosts sheltered during the exorcism scare."

Liam frowned. "Who owns the house?"

"A husband and wife. They're away traveling right now."

His brows crept up high again. "So we're going to attend an unauthorized party while the owners are gone?"

Natalie bobbed her head to the side. "Technically. I guess."

"And when we get caught and *technically* arrested for trespassing by our good friend Deputy Bekker?" he asked. "Then what?"

"That's the beauty of it. The owner came into the shop this morning and asked if I'd evaluate his book collection. He's got some rare titles he wants appraised and to possibly sell. He gave me the key and told me I'm welcome to go in anytime while they're gone. They left this afternoon."

"So you planned a ghost party," Liam said, his voice flat.

"No. The ghosts planned the party. They've been having them up there every night. But tonight, thanks to this little baby." She held up the key and let it dangle from the leather fob. "We get to go too. And I know it won't be as fun for you since you can't see and hear them all, but Gabe and Millie will be there. We can hang out with them."

He opened his mouth and then closed it again.

Finally, he said, "Sure. What the hell. Let's go to a ghost party."

Before Natalie could debate what to wear—she wanted to look good since it was her first ghost party—a knock sounded at the backdoor.

"Expecting company?" Liam asked.

"No." She frowned.

Harper would have texted if she was stopping by. And as far as she knew, Gabe hadn't developed the ability to knock. But he could push things over now, so maybe he had decided to try knocking instead of just swooping in.

She moved toward the door then stopped, glancing back at Liam. "The guy who locked me in the freezer is in custody, right?"

Liam bit out a curse followed by, "He'd better be. And if he's not and that's him at the door, we'll be putting those holes in your yard to good use. Believe me."

She did believe him as he stood and pushed past her to open the door himself.

With the freezer incident still fresh in her mind, she hated that researcher for making her too nervous to open her own damn door. She could only hope that the effects of the trauma would lessen with time.

Meanwhile, she realized they weren't in danger of

attack when she heard Liam say, "Good evening, deputy. What can we do for you?"

That was a relief. Or at least it would have been if they hadn't been just discussing the possibility of Carson arresting them for attending the unauthorized ghost party.

It was almost as if they'd conjured him.

Maybe they had. Nowadays, she didn't write anything off as impossible.

Liam stepped to the side and Carson Bekker's gaze landed Natalie. "Do you have just a minute?"

"Of course. Come on in. Is something wrong?" She remembered the bone. "Did you find something more?"

So much had happened recently, but the mystery of the bone in the backyard was still unsolved.

Carson took a step inside and his chin dropped toward his chest before he raised it to meet her gaze. "No. That's why I'm here. To tell you the search crew hasn't found anything. At least nothing bone related. There were some other things though."

He extended his arm and she saw a clear plastic bag in his hand.

"These are yours."

Liam took the bag then glanced up at her. "There's some cool relics in here."

"Great," she said without enthusiasm.

Her yard was a disaster and all she got out of it was a bag full of dirty old stuff. No more bones. No answers.

"So that's it then?" she asked.

"That's it," Carson said. "The crew from the county searched all the parts of the property that aren't paved over. Short of digging up the sidewalk and the parking lot, that's all we can do. They'll be back tomorrow to fill in all the holes, level it out and take down the caution tape. It's going to need to be seeded though or it'll be nothing but mud every time it rains."

Carson held her gaze with his sympathetic one.

"I am sorry about the mess. I can put in a request and maybe get you a check to cover the cost of the seed at least—"

"It's okay. We got it covered," Liam told him.

Carson dipped his head. "All right. Have a good night."

"Thank you," she called as Liam followed Carson to the door.

"So that's the end of that," Liam said as he handed her the bag of her questionable buried treasure. "Are you gonna be okay with this?"

"Okay with what?" she asked as she turned the bag in her hand.

Along with some loose change and a tiny metal soldier figurine was a green-tinged clear bottle. It looked old and had *Mudville* embossed in the glass. All right. She had to admit that was pretty cool. She could display it in the shop. It wasn't exactly worth digging up the yard over though.

"Are you okay with the fact they're done searching?" Liam clarified. "Are you going to be able to accept we'll never know any more?"

She shrugged and laid the bag down on the counter to be gone through better later.

"I guess. But I am excited to ponder how I feel about not getting the answers we wanted while sitting in my beautiful new formal Victorian garden." She grinned. "When can Stone get started?"

Chapter Twenty-Eight

"Being around you has always been an adventure, but I have to say this, being here tonight, might just take the cake." Liam stood in front of the large house as his gaze swept the building and its many architectural details.

The wrap around porch, now glassed in. The *porte cochère* where centuries ago carriages would have loaded and discharged passengers via the high carriage steps. Not to mention the amazing view the hilltop location afforded. There was no question, this was a gorgeous place.

Natalie had to admit she was a bit envious of the ghosts who got to be here all the time. And according to Gabe, who'd moved in here himself with Millie, quite a few had chosen to make this their new home.

She felt momentarily guilty and a bit bad for the homeowners. Hopefully they had no idea that their house had been infiltrated by the local spirits because of Natalie's panic over Harper's bogus exorcism.

"What are you doing standing out there?" Ricky called to her, sticking his head through the glass of the porch. "We need you inside. None of us can turn on the stereo. This party needs music."

"Gabe can't turn it on with his new power?" she asked.

"Gabe is a little busy, if you know what I mean." Ricky waggled his eyebrows and Natalie felt her cheeks heat at the innuendo.

"Okay. I'll be right in to do it."

The conversation had Liam turning away from the pool and the pool house he'd been admiring in the distance. He looked back to her and sighed. "And so it begins."

"What begins?" she asked.

"The conversations I can only hear half of. What are you agreeing to do now?" he asked.

"They're requesting my presence inside to turn on the stereo."

"Who is?" Liam frowned.

"Ricky." At his blank stare she added, "Gunshot wound after a card came gone wrong."

Liam nodded. "Gotcha. He was at the Halloween séance."

She smiled. "Yes, he was. See. You know the ghosts. You're a part of the community too."

He rolled his eyes. "If you say so. Come on. We might as well go in."

As they walked toward the back door, she tried to see the party from Liam's point of view. To him the house would be silent as they entered with the key she'd been given.

To her, it was very different. She could clearly hear the noise of the raucous gathering even from outside.

Inside the mudroom, two women she'd never seen before chatted and giggled until Natalie raised one hand in a wave and said, "Hi."

They froze and drew back.

"Sorry. Didn't mean to bother you. I'm a friend of Gabe's. He invited me."

Apparently they didn't feel like being social. At least not with someone alive. They swooped through the wall after a glare that left no doubt in her mind she shouldn't try to initiate any further interactions.

It was probably best to ignore the spirits she didn't know. Let them come to her if they wanted to communicate.

"Hi. I'm Liam. I'm with her."

Natalie smiled. Liam introducing himself to the ghosts he couldn't see, trying to be social, was absolutely adorable. Her heart swelled with love for this man who put up with more than any boyfriend should have to.

It made her hate to have to disappoint him. "Sorry, baby. They're gone. I guess not all spirits are excited to have a living on the guest list."

He smacked his lips. "Ah. So maybe—just throwing this out there—we shouldn't be here."

"Stop. It'll be fine. Come on." She grabbed his hand and pulled him forward.

Luckily, once Liam was in the house he was too busy looking around at the interior to insist they leave.

They moved past the butler's pantry and a coat room and into the kitchen containing the most amazing residential cook stove she'd ever seen—once the group of ghosts standing in front of it moved out of the way so she could see it.

A sea of spirits parted for them as she led Liam through the kitchen, following the sounds of the party in hopes of finding Gabe farther inside.

"Here she is! Finally. Hey, doll. The radio's this way." Ricky waved her over from the doorway.

She glanced at Liam by her side. He was busy taking in what had to be custom-built cabinetry. "The radio they want me to turn on is in the other room. Do you wanna wait here—"

"Hell no. I'll come with you," he said.

Guessing Liam didn't want to be left alone in a room full of ghosts, she hid her smile and said, "All right."

Turning, she followed Ricky through the doorway and into a room dominated by a sweeping staircase that was punctuated by two wide landings on the way up to the second floor. Hundreds of intricate wooden spindles supported the polished wood handrail.

It was like the staircase at Agnes and Harper's house, but on steroids. Like the difference between a *Grande* and a *Venti* at Starbucks. She'd love either but one was definitely bigger and better than the other.

They strode past a sofa, numerous chairs, and a fireplace in the interior room dominated by the staircase, all of which she didn't have time to really study or absorb as Ricky led her into a small, windowed room off to the side.

Inside the smaller room, furnished like a reading room with two wide leather chairs, Ricky thrust out one hand, pointing. "There."

She turned and saw the radio sitting on a low side table. "That's it?"

"Yup." He nodded. "Be a doll and turn it on for us."

She'd been expecting an elaborate stereo system with hidden speakers throughout the house and complicated controls she'd have to figure out. What she got was a small, though a quality brand, combination radio and CD player with a power button, volume control, station selector and not much more.

After one push of the power button classic rock filled the small room.

"Turn it up, would you?" Ricky asked.

Hating to change anything since technically she was here to look at books, not play around with the owner's electronics, she hesitated then finally nodded.

She raised the volume then straightened, taking a step back before he asked her to change the station. *That* she really didn't want to do. As it was she'd have to remember to lower the volume again before she left so the owners didn't get blasted when they returned home and turned on their radio. But for now the ghosts seemed happy.

At least Ricky looked happy as he said, "Thanks, doll."

Then he swooped out of the small room and disappeared around a corner to the right into an area of the house she had yet to explore.

In the center hall, which was only her guess of what the big room with the staircase would be called, more ghosts from various eras in history displaying multiple styles of dress mingled.

Some stood or sat in groupings chatting while a few started to bop to the music. One young man wearing what looked like a World War I uniform started to sing and play air guitar.

Liam was right. This might be the most surreal experience of her life too.

"Hey. You made it." Continuing the bizarre evening, Gabe walked into the room with Millie on his arm like they were the host and hostess greeting their party guests.

Liam breathed with visible relief at the familiar voice. "Gabe. Good to see...uh...I mean hear you. Oh, and hi, Millie," he added.

The girl responded with a soft, "Hello."

Gabe smiled as he asked, "This is some place, huh?"

Natalie nodded. "It sure is. Now I know why you're all hanging out here. I would too."

"There are eight bedrooms upstairs and I lost count of the fireplaces in the house. Want the grand tour?" Gabe offered.

"Are you sure it's okay?" Natalie asked.

At the same time, Liam answered Gabe saying, "Yes, please."

She turned to stare at him. "What happened to your aversion to trespassing?"

Liam tipped his head to the side. "You so eloquently convinced me otherwise... and this place is freaking amazing."

"You two ain't seen nothing yet. Come on."

Gabe led them to the other end of the spacious center hall.

"Here you've got your formal dining room with a separate entrance to the butler's pantry and kitchen area. Opposite is... I don't know what you'd call it. Music room? Formal living room?"

"Drawing room," Millie suggested softly as they all stood in the doorway staring into the large window-filled space that easily contained a grand piano as well as plenty of seating.

"Probably what she said." Gabe hooked a thumb at Millie before he pivoted to face the other direction. "And this is why you're here, Nat. Aside from the party, of course. The library. Or maybe it's an office? Either way, there's a ton of books for you to look at."

Natalie took a single step toward the room with its ceiling-high shelves filled with books that overflowed into piles on the floor and the desk. It was her mecca. A dream come true.

She was so eager to dive into the collection she considered begging out of the rest of the house tour. She turned to Gabe, the words on the tip of her tongue, when she realized there was something happening with the group of ghosts standing nearby.

Those in the immediate area had gone completely and uncharacteristically silent. When she turned, she could see why. They were all staring. At them.

Chapter Twenty-Nine

"Uh, Gabe. What's going on?" Natalie asked. "Why is everyone staring at us?"

"They're staring at us?" Liam repeated, snapping into protector mode. Standing a bit straighter, he pulled Natalie against him and looked around.

What he thought he was going to do to protect them against a hoard of spirits he couldn't see or touch, she didn't know. She was pretty sure none of his Army training prepared him for that but it was sweet anyway.

"They're not looking at us," Gabe said. "They're looking at Millie."

In nearly a mirror move to Liam's, Gabe pulled Millie closer to him defensively.

Finally, an older woman stepped forward. She looked to be of seventies vintage—both in age and era.

"I'm sorry. We were being rude." She turned her gaze to Millie. "It's just when I saw you—recognized you—I asked who you were."

"You know—knew—Millie?" Natalie asked.

"Not personally. But I was at the party. The night she…" She swallowed as the sentence dangled unfinished.

Natalie drew in a gasp as Millie gripped Gabe's hand harder.

"What?" Liam whispered.

"Someone here was at the party where Millie died." Natalie turned her attention back to the woman. "Do you know what happened? How she died?"

The woman frowned. "She doesn't remember herself?"

When both Gabe and Millie remained silent, Natalie shook her head and answered for them. "We think in cases of a traumatic…end, they don't remember the details of the actual… event."

The ghost nodded. "Well, I remember that night. I was there. I saw it all. And I'll never forget it."

"Oh my God," Natalie said as she gripped Liam's arm tight before repeating for his benefit, "She was there. She saw it all."

With her gaze landing on Millie, the woman began. "That time in history was…" She shook her head as if searching for the right word finally settling on one. "Anarchy." Glancing around the group she said, "Quite literally with all the anarchists' bombings happening."

Gabe nodded. "Especially in the north-east thanks to the Bostonians in the North End. The followers of Luigi Galleani. There were multiple events in Boston and New York. Even Hoover and his Palmer Raids couldn't stop them."

"How do you know all that?" Natalie asked.

"I told you." Gabe pointed a thumb toward himself. "Historian."

"Wait. Is that what you did for a living? Were you a teacher?" she asked.

"Yes," he answered indulgently, as if she should already know that. "I taught at a local college."

"Wow. You really are just like Indiana Jones."

After an eyeroll directed at Natalie, Gabe glanced down at Millie's face, squeezed her hand and then said to the new ghost, "I'm sorry. What's your name?"

"Harriet," the woman supplied.

"Harriet, please go on," Gabe said.

She nodded, then her gaze swept the group. "What he said was right. There were a group of guys from

Boston there at the party that night. My friend and I could see they were trouble right from the start, so we stayed clear. But Millie didn't. I saw her and her friend going into the room they were all in upstairs."

Millie's eyes widened. "I remember. The friend I'd come with was in the hallway kissing a boy, so I was alone with some of the men from Boston. They were bragging about the things they'd done and what they had planned for the future. I told them they all belonged in jail and I wasn't going to let them get away with it."

Gabe pressed his lips tight as he drew in a breath through his nose. "Oh, Millie."

With a look of sympathy, Harriet continued, "I was downstairs with my friend. We'd been dancing and were hot so we went out onto the porch to cool off." She paused. "Then we heard a thud. They'd pushed Millie off the second-floor balcony."

Natalie gasped as Gabe squeezed his eyes closed and shook his head.

"They couldn't see us on the porch from where they stood on the second floor. We were sheltered from their view. But we heard them. They were panicking. Talking about what to do with the...*body*."

She'd whispered the last word before she visibly swallowed.

"Then one of the guys with them suggested the local butcher's son. He said he knew him and that he had some gambling debts and for the right amount of money they could get him to... dispose of... her."

"Oh my God. Millie. I'm so sorry," Natalie breathed, wishing she could hug the girl. Knowing she couldn't, she looked to Gabe. "Dammit, Gabe. Hug her!"

That knocked Gabe out of his shocked stupor. He wrapped Millie in his arms and whispered against her hair.

The poor woman who'd made the big reveal looked horrified. "I'm so sorry. Maybe I shouldn't have said anything."

"No. It's good you told us," Natalie assured her before she realized it wasn't her place to do so.

"If only I could have heard it," Liam mumbled.

After Natalie summed up the story for an equally shocked Liam, the woman said, "I've lived with the guilt of that night for decades. We literally ran and hid behind the bushes of the house next door instead of doing something."

Natalie shook her head. "There was nothing you could have done."

"We could have turned them in—we saw the car they put her in drive away—but we were too afraid.

After we were sure they'd all gone, we went back in to grab our wraps that we'd left inside. That's when my friend scratched the license plate number into the woodwork of the room with the balcony they'd tossed her off, hoping someone would make the connection. But they didn't. We watched the newspapers. Millie was listed as a missing person. The horrible press even insinuated she'd run off with a man." Harriet scowled.

"Wait. Your friend scratched the license plate number of the car into the wood? One-nine-two-zero?" Natalie asked, heart pounding. She spun to Liam. "I never considered it might be a license plate. It's only four digits."

Harriet nodded. "Plates were only four digits back then."

Liam pressed his hand to her back. "Two mysteries solved in one night."

"I know!" Natalie nodded, excited until she remembered she couldn't tell anyone living about it. She turned back to Harriet. "Thank you so much. You've been very helpful."

"It doesn't seem like nearly enough, but I'm glad you think it helped," she said sadly before she moved away after one final glance at Millie.

Since Gabe and Millie were still having a moment, Natalie turned away to give them privacy and looked up at Liam. "Of all the things that might have gone down at this party, I didn't expect *that*."

Liam had his concentration face on. "You know what I'm thinking?"

"No." But she'd love to.

"If they did..." He cut his gaze to the general vicinity of where the invisible Millie stood, then lowering his voice said, "cut her up--"

Natalie's eyes widened. "The bone in the backyard—"

"Could be hers," Liam finished the thought.

"But where are the rest?" she asked.

Liam grunted. "That's the big question."

Chapter Thirty

"I hope Millie is going to be okay. She still looked upset when we left the party," Natalie said as she walked around the hood in time to see Liam pocket the keys of the Jeep he'd just parked by the lab.

He bobbed his head to one side and moved to stand next to her. "It can't be easy reliving her death again after all this time but she has Gabe. And you. And maybe she'll become friends with the lady who was at that New Year's party with her."

"Yeah. You're right. It's just so horrible. They *sawed* her into piece—" Natalie realized what she was saying and winced. Cutting up bodies was exactly what Liam did in the lab. "No offense."

He cocked up a brow as he wrapped one arm around her shoulders and took a step in the direction

of the train depot. "I use my saw in pursuit of lifesaving research. Not to hide murder."

"Yes. But it's still creepy," she reminded him.

But not as creepy as train track dude who had once again timed his nightly walk to coincide with theirs.

Natalie pressed one hand to Liam's chest to halt their forward progress. "Hang on just a sec."

"Train guy?" he asked.

She nodded.

"How long has he been here? Since nineteen-twenty do you think?"

She nodded. "Probably. He's dressed pretty old timey. Like turn of the century kind of garb. Maybe even older. Why?"

"Did you or Gabe ask if he saw anything?"

"I didn't." She avoided him as much as possible. "Gabe said he tried but got nothing. He has no jaw. He can't talk so..."

"Nat, you can get a lot of information just with yes or no answers. And I'm not talking about Madame Letisha's pendulum. Can he gesture?" Liam asked.

"I guess. I don't know. He pretty much ignores me." She'd never tried to communicate with him but she had a feeling she was about to.

"How about we try and ask him?"

We...meaning her.

Drawing back at the horror of what Liam had asked her to do, she finally nodded. "Okay. But stay with me."

After a colorful cuss, Liam said, "Of course I'm going to stay with you. I'll never leave you."

"Aww." She pressed her hands to his chest and pursed her lips. "I love you."

"Nat. Stop stalling and ask the questions." Yup. He'd seen right through her.

"Okay. Here we go." After a big breath, she turned toward train dude. "Um, hi. Sorry to bother you."

As usual, he ignored her.

Bracing herself, she stepped onto the tracks putting herself directly in his path as he continued toward her. Throwing both hands out in front of her, palms toward him, she said, "Stop! Please. I have to talk to you."

Just when she thought he would continue right through her, he stopped.

At least this wasn't a residual haunting... and she'd been reading much too much about ghosts that she even knew that term. But she guessed because he'd stopped when she'd asked, he could communicate and interact. He didn't just go through the same routine without being conscious of his surroundings. That was good.

"Can I ask you some questions and you just indicate if the answer is yes or no?" she asked, hating that this was starting to sound too much like Madame Letisha's session.

He tipped his head. She took that motion as an affirmative and her heart leapt.

"Were you here in nineteen-twenty?" she asked.

Again, he tipped his head.

She drew in a breath and glanced back at Liam. "He nodded both times."

"Nat, this is good. Keep going."

She swallowed and turned back toward the ghost. "On New Year's Eve a young woman was thrown off the balcony of a house on Main Street and killed. We think the men who did it paid the butcher's son to... cut her up and dispose of the pieces."

He nodded. More than nodded. He became visibly agitated as if trying to get his point across.

"He's trying to tell me something," she relayed to Liam.

"Then ask him a question he can answer." With a huff, Liam stepped closer to her and asked, "Yes or no, do you know where they buried her bones?"

As the ghost nodded, she grabbed Liam's hand. "He says yes."

"Then, there's only one question left." Liam's gaze

shifted from Natalie's face to the empty space on the tracks in front of them. "Can you show us where?"

This time the ghost used his one good arm to indicate they should follow him, then he started walking.

Chapter Thirty-One

They'd gathered like this before recently. More than once. A meeting of the minds.

No, not the LADS, even with the Mudville ladies' collective and individual longstanding history. But rather Natalie's handpicked cadre of those close to her.

She glanced around the individuals gathered in the meeting room. Each one had the knowledge and expertise necessary for the problem at hand...

At least she hoped they did, because there seemed to have been a never-ending parade of problems lately.

And it all began with the discovery of that darn bone.

"So, we're gathered here today to discuss Millie," Natalie began.

The girl seemed to shrink into herself at the

mention of her name, sinking back into the sofa cushion next to Gabe.

"More specifically we need to make a decision about—and I'm sorry to be so blunt, Millie—her bones," Natalie concluded, sending an apologetic glance toward the girl.

"God, how I love the smell of bergamot." Harriet, the witness to Millie's murder they'd met at the party, leaned over to sniff the cup of tea Natalie had just poured for herself.

"Would you like me to pour you a cup of your own?" Natalie asked. "I know you can't drink—but you can sniff it."

Harriet's eyes widened. "That would be amazing. Thank you."

Natalie rose and moved to the sideboard in the meeting room where a dozen mismatched teacups sat for the use of anyone meeting there. She glanced back. "Liam? Tea?"

Liam sent her an indulgent look. "Sure. Let's all have tea. Then maybe we can get back to the reason we're all here?"

Narrowing her eyes at him, she carried two cups and saucers over and then poured from the teapot steeping on the table. She pushed one cup toward

Liam and set the other in front of Harriet, who couldn't have looked happier.

"We've learned..." she began but got distracted by Liam.

After adding a heaping spoonful of sugar to the cup, he added milk until it was close to overflowing. Some very loud stirring mixed it all together before he tossed the spoon onto the table with a clatter. Then he sat frowning at the small handle on the cup that she could see his thick finger definitely would not fit in.

As she watched his indecision and wondered how this situation was going to play out, he finally just palmed the whole cup and downed the liquid in one gulp.

That done, she forced herself to focus. Where had she been again? Oh, yeah. The bones.

"Thanks to—" She turned to train track dude next to her. "I'm sorry. I don't know your name."

"Unless he knows sign language, he's not gonna be able to tell you," Ricky, aka Gunshot Wound, said from where he sprawled in the chair.

Ricky had agreed to be the representative for all the graveyard ghosts. He was of a newer vintage compared to many of the others buried there, but he was by far the most social. He talked a lot and to everyone. And in a shocking revelation, it turned out he actually listened too. He'd absorbed an enormous number of facts. Details. Rumors.

"Even if he did know sign language, do any of us know it to understand him?" Gabe asked, holding Millie's hand so Liam could hear.

A look around at the faces of those gathered led Natalie to believe the answer was no.

"Maybe he can write his name on the table with his finger? We'll be able to see what letters he's forming even if we can't actually, you know, write," Harriet suggested.

Natalie glanced at train track dude, who amazingly had accepted her invitation to join them. He sat back, a bit away from the group, in a straight-backed wooden chair, but at her question he leaned forward. He used his one hand to trace the letters T-I-M on the table. Then he leaned back again.

"Tim. His name is Tim," she announced happily to them all, particularly Liam who couldn't see what he'd written. "Okay, good. We're making progress."

"Are we?" Liam asked.

"Yes. Now hush. So, Tim has shown me all the places where he watched them bury the various..." Natalie swallowed. "...body parts. Again, Millie, I'm so sorry."

Gabe shot her a pointed glare from beneath raised brows before turning to pull Millie closer.

"The question is, what do we do with this knowledge?" she asked, looking around.

Ricky scoffed. "You keep it under your hat, that's what you do."

"Ricky said we do nothing," Natalie interpreted for Liam. "But thanks to Harriet, we know who the guilty parties are. I hate the idea they all just got away with it. It feels like we should do something."

"Babe, you're forgetting once again that you only know who they are from speaking with a ghost. You have no physical proof to show any authorities."

"We'd have the bones," she countered.

"The location of which you only know about from a ghost," Liam reminded.

"We have a license plate number," she argued.

"From a car in nineteen-twenty." Liam sighed. "Natalie, even if you could convince someone those digits are a license plate and not a year, connected to the murder of a girl everyone thinks ran away, then what? This isn't like Gabe's murder. These guys are all long dead."

Ricky pointed at Liam. "What he said."

Gabe and Harriet nodded in agreement.

"Okay, so even if we can't do anything to get

justice for Millie. What do we do about the fact that the...bones...are spread throughout the village?" God this was awkward talking about the girl's dead body while she sat right there. "Shouldn't we tell the sheriff's department so they can—"

"Fuck no!" Ricky said.

"Nat, I think you're not thinking this through," Liam said.

"I am. I'm thinking we could give Millie a proper burial so she can rest in peace." *And not in pieces...* She kept that last thought to herself. "We can't go dig up every bone but Carson's crew could."

Gabe shook his head. "And what if Carson considers it evidence? Bags them all up and sends them off to Cooperstown to be stored in an evidence locker as a cold case for the foreseeable future. What happens to Millie? Does she get yanked away with them?" Gabe asked, eyes wide.

"I don't know," she had to admit.

"Ethel and Myra's ghosts followed their bodies," Liam reminded her.

"Tough guy's right." Ricky nodded.

"I think the decision is Millie's." Harriet looked at each of them in the room. "Her body. Her choice."

Spoken like a woman who had lived, and died,

during the height of the equal rights era. Meanwhile, Millie shrank back even more.

"Millie?" Gabe asked, turning to look at the young woman tucked beneath his arm.

She shook her head and gazed up at him. Gabe leaned low and she whispered something they couldn't hear.

When he leaned back, he said, "She wants to be left alone. We leave the bones where they are and we tell no one."

"Yes. Finally. That's exactly what I've been saying. Smart girl." Ricky nodded with satisfaction.

Harriet echoed his nod and then went back to smelling her tea.

"So that's it then," Liam said. He pinned Natalie with a stare. "Are you going to be able to abide by her decision?"

Insulted she said, "Of course."

"You're really not good at doing nothing," he reminded.

"He's right about that," Gabe agreed.

"See?" Liam said, hooking a thumb in the direction of where Gabe's voice had come from.

Wonderful. Now that they could hear each other, they were ganging up on her.

"I promise you I can and I will do nothing—"

"Do nothing about what?" At the sound of Harper's voice, Natalie jumped, startled.

She turned to see Harper standing in the doorway between the meeting room and the shop as she glanced around the room. She must have forgotten to lock the front door.

"Hi. We were just talking about that garden Stone is going to put in for me. Liam is making me promise to not interfere and let Stone do his job according to the plans."

"Ooo, you are such a liar." Ricky grinned, teasing her.

"Actually, that was some quick thinking on her feet," Harriet commented.

"It wasn't bad. She's usually a terrible liar," Gabe supplied after he moved away from Millie so they weren't touching. Otherwise Harper would have been able to hear him.

Ignoring the ghost chatter, Natalie put herself into Harper's shoes and tried to imagine how things looked to her from where she was standing.

Harper did not see Harriet leaning low once again to sniff the third cup of untouched tea on the table. Or Gabe and Millie seated on opposite ends of the sofa now, both looking uncomfortable to *not* be touching for once. Or Ricky who was visibly checking her out.

Or Tim cradling the stump of his missing arm as he leaned back in the chair and observed the conversation.

Nope. Harper couldn't see any of that. What she did see was Natalie and Liam having a tea party, complete with teapot, creamer, sugar bowl, and three vintage bone China teacups for just the two of them.

That had to look weird. She should have gotten Liam a beer instead. That would have seemed more natural.

Next time... And as much as Natalie hoped there wouldn't be another occasion that she'd have to gather the ghosts, she knew there probably would if recent history was any proof.

Jumping up, Natalie asked, "What can I get for you?"

"Why don't you just tell the woman you can see us?" Ricky asked.

"I've told her that more than once. She won't," Gabe said.

"I guess I can understand that. She doesn't want people thinking she's a loon. Or a liar," Harriet pointed out.

Blocking out the ghost chatter was probably already making Natalie look like a loon. But she did her best as she moved closer to Harper.

"I actually just stopped in to ask what you want to do about the bone," Harper said.

"The bone?" Natalie repeated, a little freaked out that the ghost meeting happening under Harper's nose had been about that exact thing.

"The LADS were asking if we'll be meeting again."

"Who the fuck are the lads," Ricky asked.

Gabe went on to explain after which Harriet chimed in about what fun that sounded and how she'd like to join.

Blocking them all out, Natalie was trying to craft an answer that would satisfy both Harper and the LADS when she felt Liam's hand on her shoulder.

"That case is officially closed," he said.

Short. Simple. To the point. And, technically, true. Gabe was right. She sucked at this. She would have babbled and said way too much. Liam was a better liar then she was. Somehow, that wasn't a comfort.

Harper dipped her head. "All right. They'll be disappointed but I'll tell them."

"But maybe we could keep looking--"

"What the fuck?"

"Jeezus, Nat!"

In response to Ricky and Gabe's respective loud and ardent objections, Natalie added, "You know, for another case. We could look for a different one we could work on."

Harper nodded. "They'd like that. We'll talk about it."

"For sure." With a quick glance back, Natalie led Harper toward the exit.

But she didn't miss hearing Ricky say, "Gabe, dude, you need to tell the big guy here that he has to keep a closer eye on his woman."

"Oh, believe me. I will," Gabe answered.

Yup. Definitely feeling ganged up on.

Epilogue

THE WEATHER HAD FINALLY TURNED.

Instead of Natalie's view of the world consisting of a gray and dreary sky stretched above a brown and muddy foreground, the sun was actually shining more days a week than not.

Lawns turned green again, leaves unfurled on the trees and spring flowers had not only begun to poke their heads out of the dirt, but some had bloomed, adding a riot of color to the formerly monochrome landscape.

According to Stone, it was the perfect time to plant.

Natalie wasn't about to argue with Harper's farmer fiancé. Not only did he know exponentially more about plants than she did, but she also wanted her garden done.

By the look of the progress already made, it wouldn't be long now.

"Hey, babe." Liam looped an arm around her shoulders.

She turned from admiring the new flowering cherry Stone had planted and faced Liam.

"Taking a break?" she asked.

"Yeah, a short one. So I thought I'd come over for a little visit."

"I'm glad you did. Because there's no way I'm coming to the lab." She gave a little shudder.

Liam shook his head. "Sissy."

"Yup. And proud of it." She nodded.

In the past, visiting Liam and having to walk past Gabe's body had been bad enough. But now that Liam had won the grant he'd applied for, there were too many brains in the lab for her to deal with. Besides that, she tried to avoid being in the vicinity of the freezer where she'd almost died.

"I'm making good progress," Liam told her.

"That's great. And I'll clap the loudest when you win the Nobel Prize, or whatever you science guys get. But for now you're going to have to come here because after walking in on you and your slicing machine, I might never eat meat again."

His lips twitched with a smile. "Understood." He glanced around them. "This is starting to look good."

"It is," she agreed.

Once the pavers had been installed for the walkway, it had really begun to take shape. Now she could see the bones of her Victorian formal garden.

"And I have you to thank for it all." She turned to raise her face to Liam.

"If it keeps you busy so you don't go looking for any more bones or mysteries, it'll be worth every penny," he said, before leaning down to press a kiss to her lips.

"No kissing in the garden until it's done," Stone said walking around the corner with a square of sod.

"Not even for the guy footing the bill?" Liam joked.

"I guess I can make an exception." Stone grinned as he set the grass down then stood. "I'll have the sod put down today. I've got all we need in the truck."

"Sounds good." Natalie smiled as Stone walked around the corner again, leaving her alone with Liam. Alone until Gabe and Millie sauntered over.

"Garden's looking good, you two," Gabe said to Natalie and Liam.

"Thank you. I think it's coming out nicely," Natalie agreed.

"It is lovely," Millie said softly. "It reminds me of the gardens from my youth."

Her *youth*, which she would have for eternity since she'd died so young, but Natalie understood what the girl was saying.

Millie had come out of her shell a bit over the past couple of months, thanks to Gabe's influence. Natalie was glad of that. She and Liam could even have a normal conversation with Millie without her looking like she wanted to hide behind Gabe.

Natalie smiled and said, "Thank you, Millie. That's exactly the look I was hoping for. I'm really happy with it."

"Thank God for that," Liam grumbled.

"Amen, brother." Gabe laughed. "If Nat's not happy, ain't nobody happy."

Stone came around the corner again, arms full of sod, then stopped, frowning. "Hmm."

"What's up?" Liam asked.

Stone shook his head. "I just thought I heard people talking."

As Natalie's eyes widened in panic, Liam said, "Just us."

"Yeah, so I see. Don't tell Harper I'm hearing

voices. She'll want to bring back that sideshow of an exorcist." Stone rolled his eyes.

Natalie forced a laugh that sounded more manic than jovial. "Right? Madame Letisha. What a joke!"

Her outburst earned her various glances from both the ghosts and Liam as a large black bird swooping just a foot above their heads had her ducking.

As grateful as she was for the distraction after almost getting caught by Stone talking to ghosts, she still narrowed her eyes to glare as her nemesis settled on the edge of the roof.

Of course the crow couldn't let Natalie have even one nice moment out in the garden without disturbing her.

"Stupid crow," she mumbled as the bird started his usual deafening repertoire.

Stone glanced up. "He starts that up every time he sees the cat."

Natalie spun around to face Stone. "The cat?"

"Yeah. The black cat that's always hanging around here. That crow really hates him." Stone shook his head, kneeling to lay the sod.

"The cat," Natalie repeated. Of course. That made so much sense.

Gabe blew out a breath filled with derision. "Told you the crow wasn't a *messenger from the beyond*."

Stone's head whipped up at Gabe's words.

Judging by the looks on the faces of Natalie's companions they all realized at the same time what had happened. Gabe had screwed up. He'd forgotten to drop his hold on Millie before he spoke. And Stone had heard him.

No one moved—Natalie didn't even breathe—as they waited to see what Stone would do.

A frown settled on his face but after a few seconds and a quick glance at Natalie and Liam, he went back to single-mindedly focusing—a bit too hard actually—on the grass.

Gabe took a big step away from Millie and said, "You think he heard?"

Natalie leveled an *are-you-kidding* stare on him.

Liam glanced pointedly down at her. "I need to get back to the lab. Natalie, walk with me?"

"Sure. I'd love to." She nodded.

"Stone. Good seeing you," Liam said as he hooked his arm through Natalie's.

"Yeah, you too," Stone said, a whole lot less smiley than he'd been before.

As Liam pulled her away, Natalie glanced back and delivered a wide-eyed glare at Gabe.

Looking unhappy, he and Millie followed along behind.

Inside the lab, while ignoring the gross presence of any brain matter, Natalie turned on Gabe. "Oh my God, Gabe."

"I know. I know. I screwed up," he admitted looking miserable.

"And after all the times you made fun of me for slipping," she accused.

"What's done is done. We need to talk about what we do now," Gabe said.

"It looked to me like Stone is of the mind to ignore the whole thing," Liam said. "He made no secret that he thought Harper was hearing things and that exorcism was ridiculous. There's no way he's going to admit to hearing it too."

"Spoken like a true alpha male," she accused.

Although he might be correct. At least, she hoped he was.

"All right. So we do nothing." She glanced at Gabe, Millie and Liam. "Agreed?"

"Or," Gabe began. "You can tell Harper and Stone about us."

"Or you could do that," Liam nodded, once again in agreement with Gabe against her.

Millie lifted one shoulder and nodded too. "You could do that."

Natalie's cell phone buzzed in her pocket. She

pulled it out and glanced at the display, her gaze whipping up as she said in a panic, "It's Harper."

"Now's your chance," Gabe said.

"Are you going to answer it?" Liam asked.

"Fine. I'll answer, but nothing more." Her gaze moved from one to the other. "Understood?"

Liam lifted one shoulder. "Your choice."

"Yes, it is," she said before punching the screen to connect. "Hey, Harper."

"Natalie! Oh, my God. You're not going to believe what happened."

Her gaze cut to Liam as she asked, "What happened?"

"Stone just called me. He heard it too! He believes me now. He heard the voices. In *your* garden!"

"Oh. Wow," Natalie managed as her heart pounded.

"I'm coming over. We have to talk about this."

"Uh, sure. I'm with Liam in the lab."

"Okay. See you in a minute," Harper promised.

"Okay." Natalie disconnected and glanced around at the others. "She's coming over."

"We heard. She wasn't quiet," Liam said.

"Nat..." Gabe said, leaving the rest of the sentence unspoken.

She knew what he wanted her to do. But she couldn't do it. She couldn't tell Stone and Harper.

Could she?

"Well?" Gabe asked. "Natalie, she'll be here in a minute. What are you going to do?"

Liam frowned. "Hey, back off. Give her time to think. It's her choice." His hand on her shoulder as well as his support was a comfort when she needed it most, until he said, "But just for the record, I agree with Gabe. You should tell them."

Crap.

Harper was going to arrive and want to talk about Stone hearing people who weren't there. Just like she had heard them in the attic. And Natalie was going to have to either lie to her and pretend she knew nothing about it. Or confess to the biggest lie she'd ever told.

The one she'd been telling for almost a year.

The knock had Natalie jumping. Liam reached for the knob and opened the door to reveal an excited Harper. He stepped back and invited her in with the sweep of one hand.

Harper strode in until she stumbled to a stop at the sight of the brain on the table. At least Liam had moved Gabe's body to the back of the room and covered it better than he used to.

She made a wide berth around the brain and

rushed forward to Natalie. "Can you believe it? Stone heard it too. Do you think the spirits left my house and moved to the train depot because of Madame Letisha?"

Unseen to Harper, Liam rolled his eyes behind her.

Natalie was the one to clear the ghosts out of the village so they'd been safe. She was the one who dealt with them on a daily basis. Yet Harper was still giving that fraud Madame Letisha credit she didn't deserve. Not one little bit.

"I'll have to call and tell her it worked. She asked the spirits to move on and they did." Harper cringed. "But Natalie, I'm so sorry they chose to move to your place. I had no idea that might happen. Let me pay to have her come back and cleanse your shop and garden."

Freaking Madame Letisha.

More than a little annoyed, Natalie drew in a breath. She hated all her options, but it was obvious what she had to do.

Clearing her throat, she said, "Harper, I have something to tell you..."

"Mudville" by Cat Johnson inspired by Unadilla, NY

Behind the Book

I had no plans to write Cadaver Lab 2. To be fair, I hadn't planned on writing the first book either but here we are. It wasn't until I first heard those two words—cadaver lab—that I became obsessed with the concept.

So what's in this second book that was burning inside me until I had to get it out?

For one, the numbers—1-9-2-0—scratched into the woodwork of the bedroom with the balcony in the book are real. There is no murder attached to them (I hope) but the numbers are there. I discovered them shortly after moving into this house and have been waiting, wondering what to do with them—story wise —ever since.

In real life I have no idea who scratched the numbers into the doorframe, when, or why.

I've always imagined it happened on the New Year's Eve that 1919 turned to 1920 to mark the beginning of a new decade. That was the kernal of the idea for the party in the book, but it grew so much larger from there.

As for the rest of the story in this book, you might remember I left Natalie, Liam, Harper, Jules and Taco with the unexplained discovery of a mysterious bone. I did that not because I planned to write a sequel, but because I wanted to show that Natalie's life was never going to be completely normal. And she was okay with that.

But that left me starting book two with this random bone to deal with, which turned out to be a good thing. As I decided the details—how it got there, who it belonged to—the story of Millie started to take shape. And I'm so happy it did. I love her and that I could give Gabe his own happy ever after.

As for more fact versus fiction…

The CTE research Liam speaks about is real, though the grant he applied for is fiction.

The historical aspects—Prohibition, and the Boston North End anarchists and bombings—are fact. The big party the anarchists attend is fiction.

And finally, the evil Blue Jay nesting over the back door that Harper described attacking her and Stone was real. The nesting pair terrorized me and my husband last Spring. There was bloodshed (they hit my husband in the head pretty hard more than once) but we waited it out. Finally mother, father and baby birds left and peace returned to the backyard. The umbrella remains by the back door for defensive purposes. We are now vigilant to nip any future nest building in that area in the bud immediately.

I hope you loved my second attempt at bringing romance to the cadaver world. Will there be a book three? I honestly don't know so I'll leave you with a solid maybe.

Cat

The Graveyard Secrets Series

BY CAT JOHNSON

CADAVER LAB: A romantic comedy...with corpses

CADAVER LAB 2: Ghostly Hearts & Body Parts

CADAVER LAB 3: Spirited Shenanigans

CADAVER LAB 4: Grave's Anatomy

About the Author

A top 10 *New York Times* and nine-time *USA Today* bestselling contemporary romance author, Cat Johnson writes hot alpha heroes (who often wear cowboy or combat boots) and the sassy heroines brave enough to love them.

Known for her creative marketing, Cat has sponsored bull riding cowboys, promoted romance using bologna and owns a collection of cowboy boots and camouflage for book signings.

She writes full time from a Queen Anne Victorian in a small town in upstate New York suspiciously like Mudville where she tends to her backyard chickens and too many cats. Learn more at catjohnson.net.

Get book news and subscriber exclusives. Join the newsletter list at catjohnson.net/news or scan the QR code.